GOSSIP GOONS 'N GALS

GOSSIP GOONS 'N GALS

A novel of suspense

Lou Korus

Brookins Books LLC

First Brookins Books Printing 2018
Cover by John Toren
Copyright Lou Korus 2018

Acknowledgements

Thank you to my readers whose input and suggestions were gratefully received:

Jan Biery, Theresa Zirwes, Joanne Mellin Pat Kissel

My publisher: ***Carl Brookins, Brookins Books, LLC*** - without whom my imagination would have withered on its synapses never to be out in public view.

All my dear friends whose words of encouragement have given me reason to dream up characters with whom I love to dance, and of course, tell you about.

R. Bookmark, new and used bookstore, Youngtown, AZ, who let me get my foot in the door and agreed to have me there for a book signing and encouraging me to branch out further.

This story was made possible by the experiences I've paid for at rental communities located throughout several states. The diversity of views of residents and management styles gave me endless ideas for fictional characters I hope to meet in real life. Or maybe not. You decide.

-Lou Korus

CHAPTER ONE

"There's a body here!"

I'm thinking, there are old people living here, folks. Anyone could have been startled enough to fall over for Pete's sake! Get a grip. Stuff happens.

Then a noise to beat all noises screamed throughout the entire building, resulting in a pit forming in my stomach. It is signaling an end of a life in this apartment complex; a shriek so loud and constant my eardrums are vibrating. It's the fire alarms. Residents are coming out from within the corridors. As they flow out, strobe lights in the hallway cause them to shield their eyes. Me, I've got my fingers pushed into my ears. The clamor is deafening. I close my eyelids against a strobe light's glare radiating out from the hallways. I wish I had my earplugs.

"Management says to clear the building," someone shouted.

While residents pour out of the hall, I see Barney Smith dressed in his worn white sleeveless undershirt and boxer shorts. Same outfit he had on when they tested the alarms two months ago. There he was, in his finery, gazing around as if he'd find a flock of elderly persons in similar garb. I turn away; his skinny boney body, tall as he is, would frighten a Halloween ghost when the Arizona sunlight finds its way to shine upon his tiny, balding head. His wife, Martha, is not far behind, her housecoat buttoned up askew, her feet fitted with flip-flops slapping against the pavement outside. Her permed hair stays firm against her scalp challenging any breezes to dare move one tight curl. It must reassure her she will always appear ready for however a new day may present itself, no matter how she looks.

My eyes widen as I witness Barney moving much too close to water still pouring from the ceiling. What will happen if he becomes soaked? I don't want to see his underwear plastered against his scrawny, skeletal body. His wife Martha shouts a warning to him, too late. In his attempt to heed her call, he walked right under the waterfalls of complete embarrassment. Oh, dear. Will I ever be able to erase this tableau from my brain? His personal parts, ribcage, skinny arms, and knobby knees now exposed, causes a stir. A man next to him removes his shirt and ties it around Barney's waist. How thoughtful. Barney looks as if he doesn't understand why he did it. Others are averting their eyes, looking to the person next to them to show their dismay. A bunch of people, wide eyed.

That's what I see. I am thankful not everyone will have this picture etched in his or her memory.

People are congregating on the sidewalk several yards out from the building and are recounting Barney's experience. Residents who own dogs wear expressions of concern for their little family additions. Many kinds of small dog breeds are present. Several pooches show distress caused by the alarm noise. Others stand near their owner's legs, trembling, and looking up at their masters in search of comfort. Some are busy sniffing the backsides of other four-legged creatures tethered by their master's leashes.

Out in the alcove, a drop of something hit my forehead and I looked up to try to locate its source. The sun reflects bright and hot off the windows of the cars parked out front, so I know it can't be raining. Then a burst of wet poured all over me, like a cold cascade that follows when your shower's hot water runs out, dousing my clothes and my cart. That's when someone hollered about a body downed on the second floor.

Emergency sirens are pushing over-excited air in all directions and blaring in the distance. Fire alarms are still going off, causing chaos within each being it reaches. I suppose it is necessary because some of us oldies are not sharp in the hearing department. It's upsetting, I have to tell you. People don't know what to do.

I try to calm down. I've reacted to the commotion of the oncoming vehicles with sirens blaring. My heart is beating faster than usual. I left my cart in the alcove near the elevator. It has nothing I eat in it anyhow. It's a twenty-pound box of cat litter. I make it to the office and know I am damp enough I'd wet the upholstery chairs, so I stay away from them and perch on a plastic chair. I get my comb out of my purse and push my curly white hair into shape. Remember those waves they used to wear in the twenty's? I imagine I appear something like that. I exhale a deep sigh. Wonder how long this is going to last? Who could have dropped over on the second floor? I looked around the main room in the clubhouse. No one's in the office to give out info. I'll bet the building manager is outside waiting for the emergency responders.

I hear heavy engine noises of a fire truck as it roars past the gates at the front of the property. I know its sound by heart. They make a run to our complex two to three times a week and this place is not an extended care facility. By comparison, I don't think a UPS truck has any insulation around whatever mechanical parts are firing on their vehicles. Or, could it be an exhaust pipe rattling against the frame? I'm not sure. It sounds as if bunches of little explosions are blowing up one after another. Federal Express trucks are quieter. They must have better lubricated engines. Each vehicle has its own distinctive sound. At least emergency sirens aren't blaring anymore. A firefighter enters the office and goes to a wall where he is out of my view. I watch him leave. The building's alarms have stopped. He must have turned them off.

CHAPTER TWO

As a female, 76 years of age, I restarted my life in a city where people aged fifty-five and older live. I say restarted, because I am the primary income client for '*Worldwide Moving Vans Anywhere You Want To Relocate, Inc.*' and I have moved and resettled more times than I wish to count. I love change; crave it. Even at this age, I can't be positive this community is *IT*.

Everyone calls me Dee. My given name is Delores Ruth Anderson, nee Brooks. I'm considered short, not overweight, only round in places that aren't toned. I'm blue eyed with bright white hair. I've never had major surgery, and do not suffer from terrible maladies.

I live in Daystar city, Arizona, which is a lovely warm place of palm trees, swimming pools, and recreational centers with churches, hospitals, clinics, doctors' offices, health centers, and thrift stores. There are shopping experiences available to fill every need. Drip systems have replaced sprinklers to conserve water usage and solar panels adorn roofs and parking areas to supply power to entities with high usage. Decorative rocks have replaced most of the green grass lawns. Impending water shortages will need all properties, one day, to change over to eco- friendly plantings.

Condominium neighborhoods and single-family homes are scattered throughout several square miles of an area once devoid of human encroachment. There are rental dwellings sprinkled throughout. I live in a five-story complex called Winter Gardens, with two hundred other occupants and another two hundred dwellers in smaller buildings throughout an area that used to be a vacant and overgrown piece of land. Here, hundreds of separate lives exist where the rental payment trough is the only thing they have in common. To live hereabouts, you accept that you are near someone at the end of life. If it does not happen today, it will, in a short time. It is a guarantee.

Now that you know a little about me and where I live, I will get back to what took place when I came home from shopping when the fire alarms went off.

When I used the elevator to go up to the fifth floor where I live, it heaved with a loud thump as I traveled upward with my cart filled with one large item. I'm used to the loud clunk of the machinery; others won't deal with the lift and find it frightening. I was perplexed when it stopped moving. After a few seconds, it moved once again but in the wrong direction. The floor indicator light was not

11

working and I could feel I was descending, not ascending. When the door groaned open and daylight seeped in, I stepped out and pulled my cart with me. I was on the ground floor where I began.

When there is an emergency evacuation, I can't take my cat out into this sea of canines without putting him in a carrier. His body goes stiff, his back claws extend, and he's impossible for me to hold onto. If the alarm sounds he dashes to seek shelter under my bed, and should there be an actual fire, I'd never be able to coax him out from under there and into the soft-sided container I bought for his trips to the veterinarian.

I decided to move away from the area. I'm soaked and my head is pounding. It's bad enough I have tinnitus. Before I made my way to the sidewalk, I heard a scream from the second floor and then an added clamor assaulted my eardrums. I headed for the office, walked out of the alcove onto the sidewalk, moving fast just to get the heck out of there.

When I got to the clubhouse, I looked around and I realized I was alone. I gratefully sank into a nearby chair when down and my cell phone rang. The screen shows Mary, my close friend, is calling.

"Where are you?" she asks.

"The office. You?"

"By my car. Do you want to go to the Curly Que for ice cream?"

I laugh. It's a logical question under the circumstances. Ice cream sounds quite soothing.

"Sure. I'll be at your car in a second. I'm a little damp," I tell her.

"It's okay. Nothing will hurt the fabric in this old car," Mary says.

We get into her car, creep slowly past the fire truck. The men are taking out brooms from somewhere inside the vehicle. To sweep water, I think. There's an ambulance behind the fire truck with its back doors open and the EMT's are pulling out a stretcher. Good. The poor soul downed on the second floor will get attention.

We slunk out the front gate. There are people everywhere. I say slunk, because residents are looking at us like we are fleeing, and they, by God, have to stay. We slouched our shoulders and sunk our heads into our breast bones as far down as we could get them. No need to give anyone a full view of us, the escapees.

We drove in silence to the ice cream shop. It's our unspoken pact. No distractions while driving.

We walked into the ice cream shop and Mary and I ordered our ice cream cones, selected a booth, and sat, grinning at each other.

"You look hilarious. Where'd you get that hair do?" she asks.

"Funny you should ask. I would say the same to you."

"Oh, ya. I kinda ran, well you know my feet, walked as fast as I could to get out of there and I was napping when the alarms went off. Have you got a mirror?"

We fixed ourselves as best we could manage, but my waves had set hard, what with the hairspray I'd used to hold it in place. Mary looked fine. She has nice, manageable hair and does a good job cutting it herself to save money. I don't wear mine as short and don't trust myself to cut it. A little lipstick helped our appearances.

"This is good ice cream, huh?" I commented.

"I got the raspberry. Yours good?" Mary asked.

"I can smell that fruity stuff over here. Ya. This dark chocolate is great," I answered.

We discussed the situation at our place and concluded that it was a water problem, nothing more and that someone got a little over excited.

"Barney got soaked," I said.

"No. He didn't."

"Yup. It was, how do I put this? Disturbing. Fortunately, a kind person took off their shirt and tied it around Barney's waist."

"Ha," Mary replied. "I wonder if the man in the palm tree saw Barney?" she added.

"Doubt it. That tree is too far to the left of the main building," I answered.

The man in the palm tree needs explaining. Tilly Bauer, a darling, sweet, and caring woman, claims there is someone living in the palm tree that rises above the office building in our complex. She says he swings about and made a sort of nest for himself. Some residents fear she is seeing things or making up stories for something to talk about. Personally, I doubt she is the sort of person to make it up something this bizarre.

"Whose body was on the second floor?" I asked Mary.

"What body?"

"I heard someone yell from the second floor, *there's a body here.* Well, no. They screamed. Idiots. Somebody slipped or tried to move too fast and tripped. Who knows?"

"Think we can go back?" she asks.

"Got a number for the office? Call 'em and see if it's all clear."

Mary called the manager and reported. "Nope. Ronald says the Sheriff's there and everyone's supposed to return to their apartments and stay there."

"Huh. Wonder what's going on. Should we go back?"

"Nah. He didn't seem to think there was any rush. Said we could wait another hour."

"The consignment shop is near. Let's go shopping."

"Are you dry?" she asks.

"Oh. Well, almost. I'll walk to the store and let the sun finish me up."

We walked through the shop, oohing and ahhing at all the nice, pre-owned furniture and expertly staged living and bedroom settings. Mary pointed out some pictures on the walls. She has an expert eye for color and knows how to put objects in their appropriate places. Me, I buy what I like which is a variety of styles.

The sales clerk smiles as she makes her way toward us. "Anything I can help you find today?" she asks.

"We're just looking. You may have something I need," Mary explains.

The woman turned toward me. "Interesting way of wearing your hair. Is it hard to fix like that?" she asks.

I turned on my sweetest expression, my eyes opening wide. "Why, thank you, and no, not difficult," knowing it wasn't a compliment she was handing out this afternoon.

I swiveled around giving Mary the direction we should head with a roll of my eyes toward the exit. It's a silent language reserved for intimate friends.

While we are driving back to our place, I notice rows and rows of condominiums lining the curving streets. These have windows at the front and back and none on the sides as they are all connected. I refer to those types of homes as 'burrows for the elderly'. Indigenous prairie dogs, which live in the desert, and live similarly, make holes in the ground, one going in and one going out. In the sections of the city where there are single-family homes, there are dwellings made of adobe bricks, comprised of earth, clay and straw, with windows set back in their frames shielding occupants from the blazing summer sun and torrential rains that come with the Monsoon season about end of June.

A golf cart with its sun-browned occupants is driving on the road to the right of us in their designated lane as we slow down to arrive at the gates of our paradise.

17

The people who play golf often find their skin turns a darkened color of brown, complete with scales and tough layers that rebel against any application of moisturizers. Some folks have ravages of skin cancers removed, they hope, forever. They play more for fun and social interaction than competition; however, there are leagues that have nothing but serious players.

One of our residents, Manny, told me the word golf is an acronym for Gentleman Only Ladies Forbidden. I told him the next day he was wrong. I Google subjects I question on sites that verify the truth of things. He has a propensity for spreading unsubstantiated rumors and has a way of making them sound truthful. Manny's physical attributes are numerous; a well-tanned body, muscular, tall enough a gal can wear heels, wavy thick white hair and a smile that would charm a rattlesnake off your patio. I wonder if his wife minds his wandering eyes.

Paradise for me and my friends is a view of the beautiful sunrises and sunsets, warm swimming pools and spas, exercise equipment that works on nothing higher than 'moderate', elevators instead of stairs, occasional card games, one level living quarters, no bugs, and some folks who have something to say other than who's doing what, or sometimes, who's doing whom. A challenge, but my friend,

Mary, with her kind heart and intellectual attributes, keeps me in check. I like to identify who's doing what to whom. Not that I want to broadcast it. I just want to know.

Happy retirees, who live in the southern most areas of the desert, find pleasure riding dune buggies. I think they may be trying to escape the inevitability of their demise, breaking limbs and scraping shins as if to rail against the sureness of death or obscurity and bent on pickling their livers. My doctor has told me his concerns about pickling.

My cart with the box of cat litter is still sitting outside the elevator on the first floor when Mary and I returned to the complex. I wheel it into the elevator and once again listen to the groan and thump of the mechanical box that takes me to the fifth floor, thankful it is working again. I push the cart down to my door. There's a paper taped to it. It reads: "If you have any information regarding Jane McCarthy's fatal accident, please call the Management office at 555-625-5000." The phone number was printed in large bold letters, for those of us with compromised eyesight. In my case, not. My cataracts were removed last year.

I can't believe Jane McCarthy is dead! They're calling it an accident. I always thought she'd be the one to watch out for, that she'd off anyone who crossed her. Mary will be unhappy to learn of her death. She's the one person in this whole place who maintained a relationship with her.

This isn't something I can leave alone. I'm the 'Google Queen' as I mentioned. If I want to know answers to my questions, I find it on my computer. I am not confident it will tell me anything about Jane but I believe I can find out what police procedure would be. I'm the one who found the underlying cause of the junk in the bottom of the pool and how it got there, all because I bothered to investigate online. Seems the chlorine was not doing its job. Now, I want to learn what comes next in the impending death investigation.

CHAPTER THREE

Jane McCarthy lived on the second floor of the #1 building we call The High Rise because it's higher than the other buildings within our complex. Her apartment, located on the end of the wing, overlooks the mountains to the south. Each floor has elevators placed in-between an alcove dividing two wings. She's closest to the main road that goes west and east toward connecting highways that go to Mesa. I mention the roadways because it is often the subject of her primary complaints at social hour.

Each morning around 10:00 a.m. a few residents gather for coffee in the activities building. The attendees vary, but Jane is there daily. She needs an audience, no matter how limited.

I left my place one of those mornings a month before the water emergency incident, to pick up my mail from the Post Office box. More people than usual were sitting at two tables chatting. Mary was there and waved a hiddie-ho. I filled up my cup and joined the group. I got there, in perfect time, to miss the ailment discussions. The smell of well-brewed coffee encompassed the room. The women were dressed in hot weather wear, looked

21

comfortable in their capri pants, we called them pedal pushers when I was growing up, and sleeveless blouses. A couple of women to Mary's left were sporting extravagant outfits. Residents taking blood thinners, or the chilly willies, as I refer to them, wore a light sweater to ward off the air conditioning that cools management to an undesirable degree. The men wore shorts and tennis shoes, were neat and unremarkable.

Tilly was there that day and she repeats her notion about the man in the palm tree. Some had not heard this story. I noticed Jane's eyes rolling upward and she heaved a sigh and moved to a small table away from us.

"Which palm tree is it, Tilly?" one asked.

"The one just to the left of this building," Tilly responded, her eyes bright with anticipation.

"Let's go out there and you show us," another suggested.

The two tables cleared and everyone went outside to view Tilly's claims.

"I don't see a danged thing up there!" someone yelled.

"Who in the world would climb up there, anyway?" another asked.

"Anybody have a pair of binoculars?" someone asked.

"Tilly, exactly where is this person, up there?" I asked.

"See, he's not there right now. He usually goes up just as the sun sets," she answered.

"Oh. Okay. Guess now isn't the best time to view, huh." I replied.

"No. But as I live and breathe, I'm telling you, someone is living up there at night," Tilly said.

"We'll have to come to your place one night to see what you see," I told her.

"Yes, you will. Then you'll believe me," she said, smiling her sweetest and nodding her head in agreement.

We reentered the community room and reseated ourselves. Jane got up from the table she'd moved to and rejoined us.

I sat across from Mary. Her eyebrows raised and her eyes took a left while her head stayed in place. I realized she wanted me to get a load of Jane. Oh my. She's a lot younger than the average age of the people who live here, and lovely. She wears the type of clothes that most of us gave up in our twenties. Well, it is July and it is sultry today, but her bazooms are precariously bouncing from side to side, and up and down as she regaled her complaints and opinions. She never sits, always stands. I think it elevates her feelings of superiority. Her long dyed-red hair flips close to the face of the gal seated closest.

"They should build up that wall at the south end of the building if you ask me. The traffic noise on that street would frighten a fly." Whoosh, her hair moves to the right again.

My eyebrows went up and I looked in her direction. My guess was she didn't know flies are deaf. I think she realized her gaff, because her subject matter changed dramatically. Her long red hair followed the circling of her noggin all around to the left and back.

"Why you would even consider going to a speed dating event is beyond me," she said to Darlene Madigan.

Darlene, who is an attractive and an active senior, claims to be 80 years old. I don't believe it. She looks better than most of us who are in our 70's. She's quick to respond to Jane, her voice firm with conviction.

"I like men. I want to hear their opinions, not just the ones I have formed in my mind. I want to be able to go with someone to the movies, or dances, or go over to the pickle ball courts and play a game or two."

"You can do that with anyone. Men ain't worth your time, I'm telling you. I've been married five times and every one of them was an asshole. Of course, I'm a bitch, but none of them had the balls to cope with it," Jane said.

She laughed No, she cackled. I'm thinking witch, not bitch, the way her eyes shone with a glare and brows raised upward as I imagined the hair on the back of her neck doing the same.

There was a collective look of surprise and widening of the eyes at Jane's latest revelation. One lady turned to the gal next to her and mouthed the words 'five times', her eyebrows almost colliding with her hair line. I smiled a little at Mary and I saw the rise and fall of her chest as she sighed.

Jane touched her nose as she talked, her body tilted to the right with her right foot pointed toward the door.

"I'm an expert when it comes to men. Plenty of experience," she said patting herself on the butt. "Get it?" she finished as she turned and left the activity center, but not without blessing us with another of her outrageous and loud squawks.

That's Jane. She enters a room, commands it for a short while, and revs up the emotions of several folks. I'm sure she knows gossip will ensue when she exits. All eyes are on her as she leaves, except mine.

I choose to look somewhere else, as if to show I am not in any way affected by her revelations or dress. On the walls are pictures of various outdoor scenes, but none of the usual southwest desert scenes one might expect. It was then I noticed something new on the bulletin board. I laughed aloud.

"Holy cow! Who put that up?" I asked, after I read the bold lettering on the sheet of paper. It read, *Today's Organ Recital Has Been Postponed Due To Lack Of Interest*.

A few laughs, guffaws, and snickers erupted after I read it out loud.

"I have no idea," Martha said in her shame on you kind of voice, interrupting the laughter. "What a terrible thing to put up there. Who would do that?"

You can't imitate that woman's voice. It's as if everything she says is a pronouncement of extreme inappropriateness or exaggerated wrongdoing by the person under discussion. She needs an emery board for her sharp tongue.

"I don't get it," piped up little Margie. Her diminutive voice matches her size. She's no more than four foot six, is ninety something, and as cute as a six week old kitten.

"You see, Margie, it's referring to our discussions about our latest ailments, otherwise known as our organs. Someone, apparently, doesn't want to hear it," Mary explains.

Giggles and nudge, nudge, snort, snort spread from chair to chair. Little Margie's small bosom shook with delight when she learned the meaning of the phrase.

"I'll bet 'The Terminator' put that up," offered another.

She's talking about our resident activity director who has a reputation for spoiling our games with her acerbic remarks and rebukes.

"Should it read, Don't Ask, Don't Tell?" I said.

Nobody laughed. I shrugged my shoulders.

Discussion centered on the latest gossip. It reminded me of when we played 'telephone' back in the day. We'd sit in a circle. The first person tells a 'secret' to the person seated next to them whispering it into their ear. They pass it on until the last person has heard it who repeats what they heard out loud. The news never ends the way it started out.

I listened as the conversation volleyed about the room from person to person.

"John Hammer is going to the rest home," someone said.

"No, he isn't. He died."

"He didn't die. He had a stroke. His wife can't care for him because she had a heart attack, so they are both going to an extended care facility."

"She died?"

"No, no. Nobody died."

"Oh. I thought you said he died."

"So now they're broke?" another asked.

"Hammer died and all the money's gone," another offered.

"Bunny's gone?"

Many of the coffee drinkers look confused.

Oh gadzooks. I butted into the deteriorating conversation, spoke slow and distinct. "John had a stroke. He's not broke. He and his wife are both going to a care facility. Bunny's fine. My neighbor's cat, Bunny, is just fine."

"Oh. I see," a community of heads bobbed in understanding.

There's a small pause as drinkers pick up their coffee cups and press them to their lips.

I decide to interject a different subject.

"Did I ever tell you about the time the engineer from another department came up to my desk at work?" I asked.

I watched as they nodded 'no's'.

Before I began, several of the women decided to tell about their former careers. This is a regular occurrence; the interruptions in conversations, while some take a moment to talk about their former lives. It must be important to them to relate their experiences as several are now widowed, alone and wondering what their new role may be and how better to distinguish themselves than to talk about episodes in their lives before coming to this retirement community. I'm no exception.

Willy brought the conversation back to me.

"No, Dee. What's your story about the engineer? I want to hear it. I was an electrical engineer, you may recall."

"Yes, I do remember, Willy. Well, here goes. The guy has papers in hand when he comes to my desk and asks me for a clipper pape." I laughed, remembering how a friend of mine often screwed up words like that. "I told him

I understood what he had just said. Then he continued. "Well, that's not the worst I've ever come out with," he explained. "One time, I went to the bank, and when I got up to the teller's window, I asked the woman if she would shesh my cack." I said to him, "Wow. That was a doozy. I hope you weren't wearing a raincoat with nothing on underneath!"

"Good one, Dee," Willy said.

The table of coffee consumers erupted with laughter when they figured out the engineer's mistake.

It wasn't long after the laughter died down that the gossiping resumed.

Jackie started the chatter with a post-menopausal bass tone in her voice. "I heard Manny is divorcing Barbara and moving in with Jane."

A collective, "Huh?"

"Yes Ma'am. Jane's been hustling him from the day she moved in here. You should see what goes on at the pool at night when they think nobody's watching," Jackie added.

"Really," I say. What do you know? A rumor that Manny didn't start. I'm one of the people at the pool most nights. Must not be late enough for whatever she thought was taking place.

"Jackie," Mary began "I know you don't want to be the person who tells things about people that aren't true."

"I'm telling you, it is a fact I heard that," Jackie answered accentuating the word 'fact'.

Wow. She heard it so now it is fact, whether true or not.

"What's happening at the pool?" Margaret asked. "Someone pee in it again?"

"Jane said they did," someone answered.

"Who did?" Margaret asked.

"And smoking cigars," another added."

Oh brother. I'm out of here. I gulped down the last tepid dregs of coffee. "Listen folks, it's been lovely, but I've got to get back and see to my cat. He's been acting strange, lately."

"Is he sick? I know a good vet, Margaret offered."

"Thanks, but I think he'll be fine. He may need some exercise and attention."

Mary got up and walked out with me through the French doors leading to the courtyard. They open wide enough to ensure wheelchair occupants will be able to negotiate the space without difficulty.

I complimented her on her choice of clothing for the day. She has a talent for choosing great colors that compliment her ivory colored skin stretched tight across her high cheekbones. Her delicate flowery blouse added a touch of blush to her face. I admired the shine of her complexion and the lack of wrinkles. Her small frame traversed the sidewalk with the ease of an experienced model; her feet enveloped in a high-end brand of walking shoes purchased from any one of the numerous thrift stores in the area.

Out of the building, I turned to Mary. "Is it me, or are more people trying to get on the diminished hearing list?"

"Just one of those days. Lots of people talking at once. Acoustics in that high-ceilinged room aren't the greatest. I'm going over to Jane's for a while. She seemed agitated this morning before everybody got there. I think she needs someone to talk to. You probably realized this yourself, but she's not very well educated. Smart, but no book smarts."

"Ya. Can tell the way she talks. Smart? I don't know. Anyway, don't forget your counselor's hat. See you later at the pool."

I squeezed her arm before she turned to go on her way. Mary's such a good person. Never believes what she hears at coffee time. She waits until it is uttered from the mouth of the originator to decide its veracity.

***

The pool is where I first met Mary and Janet. I was the new resident and they welcomed me into their circle. We spent evenings talking about our past lives, and the careers we enjoyed. We also compared notes about how we were raised, each of us originating from different areas of the United States. The similarities brought familiarity; the differences brought a wider view beyond ourselves.

It is six p.m. and Mary, Janet, and I went to the pool for our nighttime cool down. July temperatures are always upward of 100, thus waiting until the sun goes down is the best time for a dip. Janet wore one of her designer swimsuits, ivory colored with a turquoise flower gracing her left boob with a matching cover-up that flows out to her thighs. Never mind she's big boned. Janet is tall and carries her skeleton well. She's so Italian that you're afraid to hug her hard because you're sure the marinara sauce will leak out from her armpits. She's a southern Italian since she grew up in Georgia and like Mary and me, a widow. Unlike us, she has tons of money. Lives in a poolside unit furnished with authentic Italian pieces and her original

33

paintings of scenery make you feel as if you are there. The heavy gold and red Italian fabric draped about her windows are soft and velvety and serve as a barrier to the sun that shines in from the west window. The dark furniture glows with wood nourished with oils. I bet she pays as much for a pint of furniture oil as I do for a tank of gas. All the furnishings complement each other. The dishes in her china cabinet are ornate but not ostentatious. I like being in there. Not in her china cabinet, but in her apartment. It feels welcoming, restful, and rich. There's always a hint of garlic in the air when you come through the door. I can't help but think about the gourmet leftovers she has stored in her refrigerator. Then I remember that the microwave would never do them justice.

The pool is so hot that night it felt like bathtub water heated to hot tub temperatures that would alleviate a northern person's winter-chilled extremities. In spite of it, we exercised for at least half an hour. I became too warm and went to cool off on one of the lounge chairs allowing the warm summer wind to cool my wet body. They followed me.

"This is the life, huh? We say this often at night, but it's true. No better way to cool down in 100-degree evening heat than to get wet in the pool and let the light desert breezes race across our wet and exhausted bodies," Janet said.

"Listen to you, all flowery with your words," I told her.

"It's true. The spirits around us are enjoying it as well," she added.

"I'm sure." I'm *not* sure, but if she thinks so, I can at least agree. It's a nice thought.

We sat on our towels without patting ourselves dry.

"Did anybody watch the show about the brain on PBS?" I asked.

"Yes," they both answered. We discussed for quite a while.

"Made me feel like someday they'll be able to fix sick brains or prevent them from going haywire, anyway." Janet commented.

"Ya. That'd be great. Wish it could happen now. I can think of a couple of candidates who'd benefit," I added.

"For sure," Mary agreed.

"Well. Anybody have any news on the latest Jane escapades?" I asked.

"I've been talking to her on a regular basis, guys. She has issues, real issues, and I believe they're valid. Once you get past all that, she's actually fun. So, don't be too quick to judge," Mary explained.

"You're a brave soul and kind, Mary. Good for you for making the effort. Most of us need to vent to someone. Maybe that's what she needs," Janet said.

"I think so. Anyway, just let her rattle on when she gets a little unglued. I hope one day it will become less and less. She's taking steps to try to change things. We'll hope for the best," Mary said.

"Okay. We'll do that," Janet and I agreed.

"By the way, has anyone noticed how our bathing suits are fading? Since I found out the chlorine level was too low someone must have decided it was best to up the amount," I asked.

"You're right, Dee," Janet answered.

"You and your computer. Look what you've done," Mary said.

"Better than that gunk don't you think?" I said.

"I suppose," Mary answered.

"I'm going in the pool one more time. Anyone else with me?" I asked.

We're a little slow getting up out of the lounge chairs, what with all our creaks and groans associated with our common long-term acquaintance, Arthur Ritus, but once up and out of our seats, it's a different story.

The placid water once again undulated with waves resulting from three separate cannon ball jumps into the pool accompanied by three loud whoops. You can take the water out of the pool, but you can't take the kid out of the elderly.

CHAPTER FOUR

The next morning I went to the office to drop off my rent check. I saw Jane was in front of the desk talking to Ronald the manager. Ronald is quite old for an employee of the corporation that owns the complex, but sharp and intelligent. He knows all the occupants by name and has a quiet charm that serves his purposes well. He is also computer savvy and can help those challenged in that area. Jane appears to have him engaged in a confidential conversation.

I went into the library room to wait. While looking at book titles, I could hear a female voice rising and falling in volume. Thinking Jane must still be out there, I peeked around the corner. She's the lone person at Ronald's desk. She turned, saw me, and was quick to exit the front door, but not before I got a glimpse of her reddened cheeks and I saw her take a swipe at her eyes.

Of course, Ronald divulges nothing of his conversation with Jane to me as he accepted my envelope with the rent check in it. I prefer to pay my bills online but somehow I missed the deadline to do so. Hence, the hand-written check. Out at the mailbox I ran into Martha, the one with the exaggerated demeaning voice.

"Oh, hi there Dee. Did you see Jane when she left the office? Let me tell you, that woman is heading for big trouble. She had the nerve to tell my husband he is a male chauvinist pig," her rapid-fire delivery in full swing.

"Oh dear," I said as I fit my postal key into the lock. I was thinking as she spoke that you should be able to click on something in Microsoft online Thesaurus and hear her voice explaining the definition of 'scolding, with the intent to shame'.

"We all went to dinner on the bus last night. You should see how the woman behaves. Loud? The people at the next table got up and left before they even finished their dinners." Martha's mouth turned down as she glared at me, her blue hair never moving.

"I'm sorry. You must have been distressed." Her eyes were squinted and their intensity was as notable as her rebuking sounds.

"Distressed doesn't cover it. Jane started in when we got on the bus and didn't stop until we got back. I'm telling you, someone's got to do something about her."

"What do you suggest?"

"For one thing, did you know she carries?"

"Carries?"

"A gun. Yes! A gun. Was waving it around on the bus. Keeps it in a pocket at all times, according to her."

"Oh boy. Well, let's hope she doesn't find cause to use it. It's legal to carry a gun here, right?"

"I suppose. She was waving it around. Lord a livin' the danged thing could go off!"

"I hope she's careful with it."

"You couldn't call that behavior careful! Anyway, don't you think that's out of line for her to talk to my husband that way?"

"I can see it bothered you. Maybe you and Barney can find a way to—"

"Find a way, nothing! I don't ever want to be anywhere near where she is from now on."

"I understand, Martha. I hope you and your husband can manage it."

"Yes. Well, I'm telling you now. Beware. That's what. Beware." She blinked several times as if she was underlining every word.

Martha took her mail, gave me a look that would frighten a concrete statue, and left. She headed for the office, I had no doubt, to complain about Jane. The poor woman must have her hands full. What with a husband who has little modesty and has shown up in the hallways more than once in his skivvies, and can be heard barking orders to Martha if you happen to pass by their door when he's at it. Maybe she doesn't bark back at him. Maybe she's saves up all her negative energy and dumps on everybody she sees.

I walked back to my residence and took in the smell of the humid air coming in from Mexico, causing the desert to give up a slight smell of the former ancient ocean bed's fermented plants and dead carcasses. Martha had given me some thought, though. It wasn't good. I could feel something ominous might happen.

***

I played with my cat, fed him and put fresh water in his bowl, smoothed my hair as best I could and made sure my face was presentable. Not that my Mom would notice, but I cared. My mom is 96, just 20 years older than I am. Her overall health was quite good but dementia forced me to put her into a long-term care facility. She seems to do well there. Even more so when there is music. She even gets up and dances around her wheelchair when the rhythm takes hold of her brain. I love to see the look of total joy when it happens.

I kissed her cheek when I found her sitting by the window. Her hair was still pretty. The naturally curly locks had been combed and fixed to look nice and was quite flattering. To me she is one of the more attractive residents, despite her age.

"Hi Mom."

She stared back at me with a sweet smile and the bluest eyes you've ever seen. They are almost electric when she's coherent. "Who are you?" she asks.

"Mom, it's me. Your daughter, Dee."

Her head tilts as she examined my face. "Oh, Dee." There's a long pause as she formulated another thought.

"You should go to see Bert more often. He's mad at you for not visiting. Can you do that?"

"Of course, Mom."

"It's a long drive, I know, but, please make the effort, for me," she pleaded. "I think Bert must be quite old by now, because I'm 90, right?"

"Yes, Mom, that's right."

I didn't remind her that Bert is her father and has been gone for a very long time.

"I will visit him, Mom. Let's go out to the common room and see what's going on, okay?"

The activities director was helping the patients with chair exercises. The room is painted pink. I read somewhere it is a calming color and I guess, for the elderly patients with varying stages and types of anxiety, it would be a good choice. I wheeled Mom into place and watched as she struggled to move from side to side with her arms extended as far as she could reach. She's forgotten I'm there. I watched and remembered with sadness the mother who took me to endless piano lessons and encouraged me in anything I ventured to explore. It is some consolation I am confident she is living in a good place and has such great people to take care of her.

After the exercise session, I wheeled her back to her room. The empty look in her eyes returned. I wound up the music box perched on the small table next to the brown lounge chair. Mom's head tilted as she began to react and her eyes followed the ballet dancer as she twirled to a sweet waltz atop a ceramic dance floor. The tune repeated and I put words to a few of the notes: 'I'm watching you now, but no one is there'. One, two, three, one two three. I can't help myself; I began dancing about the room along with the ballet dancer. Mom laughed. She sounded musical, happy and delightful.

To pass time, I decided to say aloud what I knew about the developing circumstances where I live. Hearing it helped me decide what was important and I don't have to worry that anyone will challenge my conclusions. The one thing I decided was that I needed to talk to Mary. I wondered if she knew about the gun.

After a short time with silence from both my mother and me, I got up from where I was sitting in the small blue upholstered chair that graced Mom's living room for all the years I can remember and I helped her to the bathroom. I heard the clank of metal against china and the roll of the dinner cart coming down the hall. The aides were serving dinner so I sanitized the tray that would hold her meal. I fussed with her hair, wiped her soft sweet face with a dampened cloth, and kissed her goodbye, wishing as always, there was a better way to participate in the last days some of our loved ones spend, suspended between moments of reality and endless days of nothing meaningful. I leave a saddened piece of me behind each time I go. The pleasant faint smell of cleaning products followed me to the lobby by the front doors.

**

I turned on the radio in my car, hoping to find some good music to alleviate my pain. Brahms' Intermezzo A, played by Arthur Rubinstein, lent itself well to my mood. The pianist caressed the notes. The piece is melancholy, pensive, and at times bright. I gave in to its spell of peacefulness. I drove back through the gates of Winter

Gardens admiring the resilience of the greenery planted alongside each building. The palms were swaying gently in response to a warm July breeze; oleander blooms broke up the greenery as well as bougainvillea plants. I parked my car under the aluminum canopy. I felt the sting of hot air as I got out of my car. There was a large group of people coming up the sidewalk from the community room.

"Hi everyone. How's your day going?" I asked.

"We've been out to lunch and then a tour. Went on the short bus, to China Village. Good food. You should go next time," one woman answered.

"It's also important that you sign up for the activities meeting next Wednesday morning. If you are going to attend stuff, you need to come and put in your two cents worth," Martha said. She glared down at me, looking over the top of her sunglasses that were sliding down the ski slope of her nose. Her tone was sour and accusing.

"Good idea, Martha."

Martha stepped out from the group and took my arm. "There's a lot to talk about there, too, if you know what I mean," she whispered, while punching her glasses back up into position. She had taken time to pick out something to wear that matched, which was unusual for her.

"Nice outfit, Martha. I'll be sure to come to the next meeting."

I smiled at her and turned back to return to my apartment. I noticed the new pot of fake flowers that adorned the floor next to my neighbor's door. She is another one of the widows residing within. She did have good taste. They looked real and I smiled. As soon as I was inside my door, I turned the air conditioner on a bit lower as the afternoon temperatures outside had gone well over 105 degrees. I needed time alone to recover from my visit with Mom. She looked well, but I still found it hard to accept I can never again have a heart-to-heart talk with her. I felt the sharp stab of regret near my heart. I so miss the closeness we enjoyed over the years.

I was in need of the company of my friends. I called Mary on my cell phone. "Mary, this is Dee. Would you like to come for supper before we go to the pool? I'll call Janet, too."

Janet and Mary arrived together at 5:00 PM. I made Swedish meatballs from a recipe I looked up on my computer and decided to cook some brown rice and broccoli to go with it. I had set the table earlier, complete with fabric napkins, my good silverware and china. We ate and chatted.

We cleared the dining table and went to the living room. I would wash the dishes later, preferring to have conversation rather than chores.

"How's your Mom?" Mary asked.

"She was pleasant today and didn't appear angry about anything."

"Good. I think you made the right decision putting her there, Dee," Janet said.

"Ya. It's easy to get there and they take good care of her. I wound up the musical ballerina you two gave her and danced about her room with the music."

"You goof. Did she laugh?"

"Ya."

I changed the subject. "Mary, how are things with Jane? Martha told me she was boisterous on the short bus and at dinner the other night. Are you aware that she carries a gun?"

"Yes, and with good reason. It comforts her."

"Really. Anything else you wish to share?"

"No."

"Gadzooks woman. Why would she need to have a gun with her? I cannot imagine I would ever be comfortable carrying one. But, I guess some people are like that."

"I can't divulge what she says to me in confidence. Sorry. I'm sure you understand," Mary explained.

"Yes, Mary. I do understand. But if she's angry about whatever, I'm concerned for your safety."

"Carrying a gun isn't such a bad thing, do you think, Dee?" Mary says.

"Well, Martha said she was waving it around on the bus."

"Oh. Well. That sure is a different matter. What say you to that, Mary?" Janet asked.

"Guess I'll address that issue with her."

I saw a cloud fleet across Mary's eyes, indicating she was processing the information and tuned us out for a moment.

"Martha also told me Jane accused Barney of being a male chauvinist pig. Martha didn't much like it. She was quite upset about it."

Mary's eyes cleared and she directed her gaze at me. "Well, I can understand how she would defend Barney, well, sometimes. He must be a real joy to live with."

"An interesting couple, I'd say. Somehow, it must work for them. They've been married more than forty years," I offered.

"Wow. More than I'd put up with," Janet commented. "On another subject, I went to the activity planning meeting. It was wild. Bertha, The Terminator screamed at little Margie when she suggested we plan a picnic. She told her it was a stupid idea to have a picnic at the hottest time of the year. Margie sank down in her chair and told me she meant to plan it for October when things cool down. Of course, The Terminator didn't hear that. Jane called her out on it. Terminator glared her down. It was quite a sight. Jane backed off but didn't look too happy about it."

"That's one positive thing for Jane. She didn't blow up." Janet offered.

We thought about that for a moment.

"It's not too late for a swim," I suggested. "You guys game?"

"Sure. Let's do it."

***

The skies gave off the last of the grayish blue and pink streaks of the Arizona sunset as we put our towels on the chairs.

"Damon is out on his patio, Janet. Give him a flash of that blue flower on your chest."

"Dee. Not nice. I'm sure his wife gives him enough. She's beautiful, you know."

"Yes. You're right. I find it odd that he's out there alone every time we're down here."

"See that glass on the table next to him? I bet it's his cocktail hour," Janet said

"Janet, I like your bathing suit. It is lovely. Where'd you get it?" Mary asked.

"Gosh. I don't remember. Think I might have purchased it before one of my trips to Italy," Janet answered.

"I'd love to find something nice like that to replace this thing," Mary said, pulling at the fabric. "It's getting faded and starting to sag."

"Not unlike my skin, huh," I added. "Want to go shopping for a new one? I'll go with you," I suggested.

"Umm. Maybe later in the month," Mary answered.

"Okay. Last one in is a—" My words were drowned out by my major splash into the pool. Anyway, there wouldn't be a real race to see who jumped in last. We amble at a slow pace to any destination, taking care to negotiate any terrain that might hold unwanted consequences. It wasn't that long ago that Janet missed the curb because she was preoccupied and didn't notice it.

Nursing that long, once slim, now oversized swollen ankle was not fun.

CHAPTER FIVE

The day after Jane's death, Mary came to see me.

"Mary, you okay? You don't look so good." I said, placing my hand on her forearm as I closed my door.

"Well, I'm upset about Jane's death, but that's not the only thing. I stopped at the front desk before I came here and Ronald wouldn't tell me anything. I asked if they'd notified her family. He didn't say anything except 'I'm not at liberty to give out any information.' Didn't even apologize. I suppose he can't. Say anything, that is. Anyway, never mind that. I have a key to Jane's place. I want you to come with me.

"Why are we doing this?" Mary didn't respond to my question. She looked preoccupied, fiddling with the key. "Okay. Let's go. "

We walked down the hall, past the elevator and into the next section of units. Jane's living quarters were at the end of the hallway.

Mary opened the door and we walked in. My mouth hung open in surprise. The vertical blinds were closed, but there was enough light to see all the furniture and belongings were gone. There was a slight odor of heated dust hanging about. Mary turned on the overhead dining room light. I was stunned, not saying anything. Mary was shaking her head back and forth in disbelief. There wasn't one piece of furniture in the place.

She went into the bedroom and I followed and walked to the wall where Jane would have positioned her bed, judging by the depression in the carpet. Mary got down on her knees and ran her fingers against the carpeting where it met the wall, taking care as she lifted it up. It gave way after a slight tug and she pulled more away from the wall.

"Come 'ere."

I watched as she slid her hands under the carpet, retrieving plastic covered sheets filled with pictures.

"Huh. Would you look at that? How'd you know those were there?" I asked. There were six of them.

"She told me," Mary answered.

I held them while she continued her search and we went through each room, I could tell she was as astonished as I was at the bareness. Her mouth opened and closed frequently and she shook her head several times. I followed her into the bathroom and vanity area. There were no windows in there so I switched on the light. Jane opened a drawer in the vanity and with her hand upside down, she pulled out a small notebook taped to the underside of the counter.

"Shh. Mary. Stop. I think I hear someone coming." I turned off the light.

"Oh lordy. Where can we hide?"

"The storage room. Come on!"

We hurried out the patio door, closing it with a quick and quiet motion. I was glad the storage door was unlocked and we squeezed in next to the hot water heater. Couldn't hear a damn thing, until we heard the patio door slide open. In the dim light, I could see Mary's eyes were wide open like mine. I was shaking with fear of discovery. Mary reached over and took my hand in hers. It was cold. I knew she was frightened too.

My heart was pounding so hard I felt certain they heard it on the other side of the door.

We heard two male voices talking in low tones, but I couldn't make out any words. It sounded as if they were walking back and forth on the patio, pausing, and then the footsteps continued. I pushed air out of my diaphragm making an effort not to make any noise. At last the patio door slid shut with an audible click.

I can't say what Mary was imagining, but I was afraid they'd come back out, throw open the storeroom door and—well, I don't know. Shoot us, or something.

After about five minutes, still inhaling and exhaling without sound, we determined it was safe to come out of the storage room.

"Wait a second, Dee. Let me see if there's anyone walking around down there that doesn't live here. Or a car leaving. Yikes. Let me in there with you."

"What did you see?"

"Two men in suits walking over to where visitors park. They got in a new looking SUV and drove out the gate. I'm sure they didn't look back up here. "We're far enough away from them that I think they wouldn't be able to see us."

We both exhaled a sigh of relief. Our attention went to getting back into the apartment.

"What if they locked the patio door?" I asked.

"Oh lordy." Mary opened the screen door, tried the sliding door and found it locked. She turned and looked at me. "You've got your cell phone, right?" she asked.

"Ya. Never without it."

"Call Janet for me."

"What if someone sees us standing out here?"

"Oh lordy. Let's get back in the storage room. Leave the door open a crack so we can see. Now call her." Mary's whispers sounded urgent.

"I'm calling, okay?" Janet picked up after the first ring. "Janet, it's Dee. I need to have you talk to Mary." I handed the phone to Mary.

"Janet. It's Mary. As fast as you can, walk over to Jane's and stand down below on the sidewalk where her storage shed is. I'm going to toss you her door key and you get up here as fast as you can and unlock the patio door. Dee and I are stuck up here. No, don't ask any questions, just hurry up. And be quiet about it. Don't attract any attention."

We waited and sweated. It was getting mighty hot in that shed. It seemed like a good half an hour before we spotted Janet standing down there, looking up. Mary got out onto the patio and dropped the key. We had to wait again to see if she caught it.

"I sure hope she uses the stairs to come up here so no one sees her," Mary said.

"Ya. Holy cow it's taking forever. It's damned hot in here," I complained.

We both heard the patio door sliding open. I had a fleeting vision of two men opening the shed door and finding us there. I held my breath. The shed door opened. Janet looked as bewildered to see us in there, as we were relieved to see her on the other side of the door.

"Come on, you guys. We've got to lock up and get the heck out of here. Now, be quiet for heaven's sake, okay?" Mary instructed.

I felt my brow and it was wet. Mary had tiny beads of sweat on hers as well. I swiped the moisture off and Mary did the same.

Mary closed the door and locked it. We left Jane's taking small quick steps on our way back to my apartment.

After I closed my door, we looked at each other wide-eyed.

"What the heck?" I said. "Look at me. I'm shaking."

"What the heck, is right," Janet said. "What were you guys doing at Jane's? And why are all her things gone already?"

"I'm shaking too, Dee," Mary commented.

Mary came over to me and put her hands on my arms. "Let's sit down. Lordy."

Mary's expression looked thoughtful, her head tilted to one side as she considered her next sentence. "She died yesterday. Can you believe how it got cleaned out that fast? And why?"

"Do you have iced tea or something, Dee? I'm dying of thirst and I want some answers out of you two," Janet said.

"You're dying, what do you think we're doing, girl? Took your sorry ass long enough to get us out of there," I said. "It was damned hot in that shed." I got up from the couch. "I'll get us some tea."

I took three glasses from the china cabinet, filled them with ice cubes, poured the brewed tea, and put a slice of lemon on the lip.

"I think it's obvious you two know more about this than I do," Janet said.

"How'd you know where to look for that stuff?" I asked.

"What stuff?" Janet asked.

"Those pictures and that notebook on the couch there," I answered.

"Jane gave me precise instructions where to retrieve these if she should be hospitalized or incapacitated in any way. But, listen to this: I went in her apartment after you and I got back from the Curly Que and I'd seen the note on my door to call the Sheriff's office. I thought I should get in her place right away before management, officers, or whoever came a calling. All her belongings were in there at that time. I felt funny being in there, but Jane asked me to get some items if anything ever happened to her, so I gave a quick look around."

"You did?"

"Ya. I felt it was the right thing to do. I didn't have time to find what I was looking for because I thought I heard someone coming down the hall. I peeked through the peephole and after someone went by, I'm telling you, I got out of there. I was spooked. I figured I'd wait and have you come with me the next day. Thank goodness whoever cleaned it out didn't know I'd been there."

"Well, you think they don't know. How do we know what they know, huh?"

"And furthermore, who is 'they'?" Janet asked.

"Oh, don't scare me like that, you guys," Mary pleaded.

"Do you think there could be anything in that notebook the Sheriff or police should be made aware of?"

"I'm not sure, but we'll sort through and see."

"Okay. But, tell me. What has she told you about her life? Why was her stuff cleaned out in the dead of night?"

"I'll fill you in after we get a chance to go through what we have."

"Wait a minute. A notebook? You best give it up, girl," Janet said. "How do you suppose anybody got in there and moved all her stuff out without anybody noticing?"

"It must have required a crack team of individuals trained in stealth," I offered.

"Ya. Like in CIA or FBI procedures, or big bad government officials. Dead of night. Dark uniforms. Shoes that don't squeak. Neighbors sound asleep and too deaf to hear anything anyway. Quiet engine on a vehicle they pushed out the gate and didn't start it up until out of sight. Those sort of things," Janet said.

"What a visual," I said. "My gut tells me the persons who cleaned out her things must have careened about the space to the excited rhythms of the music from Can-Can. They left it spotless with no hint remaining of its former occupant. They must have left the building like the black winged Stealth Bomber, nary a noise, flying under the radar of inquiring minds.

"Talk about visuals! That's good, Dee, Janet said.

"Okay, very funny you guys. I think you are closer to the truth than you realize," Mary said.

"Really," I said. "What is it you know?"

"Let's start with what I found in there," Mary said.

My phone rang, interrupting the conversation.

"It was Martha," I explained. "She's on her way over. It sounded urgent. Here. Let me put this stuff in my office. We don't need to have it out where anyone can get a glimpse of it."

Martha rang my doorbell. The sight of her when I opened the door surprised me. Her bluish hair looked disheveled and she was dressed like an old-fashioned hausfrau in a flowered apron covering a red checked button-up shirt and droopy looking shorts. Her eyes were wide open and she looked frightened. The sticky strips on her sandals weren't secured and she stumbled as she made her way into the living room.

"Goodness, Martha. You look scared out of your wits. Just come in and sit down," I said.

"Oh. Mary and Janet. You're here too. Good. I need people to talk to." She wobbled over to the couch and lowered her head as she spoke, looking up over the top of her glasses while lowering her body into the sofa.

"I'm telling you I am. It's about Jane." She stopped and looked at both of us. Then she bent over and secured the straps on her shoes.

61

"Yes?" Mary asked.

Her head popped up. "I killed her." Martha confessed.

"How in the world can that be?" I asked. I put my hand over my mouth. Was I trying to suppress bad words or something else?

"Let me tell you."

"Lordy," Mary said.

There were a few long seconds of silence until she began, her chest rising and falling until her breathing slowed.

CHAPTER SIX

Three pair of eyes went to Martha's face. Martha fussed with her apron and after a struggle got it off. She pushed her bluish hair at the temples several times with the back of her hand. She began opening and closing her mouth, moistening her lips, and then she started to speak at last.

"I, well, I ran into her, well, you know, she was there when I was, in the alcove." Her voice took on the familiar accusing tone, as if it was Jane's fault they found each other in the same place at the same time. Her hands flew away from her body while she talked giving the painful revelation a place to go.

"When was this?" Mary asked.

"You know. The afternoon when the alarms went off." Her fingers wiggled with her arm flailing off to the right.

"Okay. Go on."

"I decided to let Jane have it. Words, words," she emphasized. "I didn't mean to *do* anything to her. I let her know, clearly, she had no right to criticize my husband in public. I told her she should have come to him in private if she had a beef with him. My Barney's not perfect, but he never did anything to cause her to chastise him at the dinner in front of all our neighbors. I told Jane about a lot of other things I didn't like about her too. I scared her. I know I did. Her face looked all screwed up and her mouth hung open, but she never said anything back to me. Just kept looking at me like I was going to haul off and hit her. I did keep making my point, though. I poked her in the chest each time I wanted to make sure she understood what I was telling her and how I wanted her to stop behaving like a sex-crazed dame! It was the last sentence that did it."

"Did what?" we said in unison.

"Jane. She dropped over. Dead. You see? I killed her." Martha looked as if she'd condemned herself to the gallows. Both of her arms flew up as she spoke.

"Lordy," Mary said. "You couldn't have killed her by poking her in the chest. It's not possible, is it?"

"Naw," Janet said. "Someone must have slipped her some poison earlier and it finally tipped her over at that exact moment."

"Good heavens," I said. "This is almost funny. You poked her, how hard, Martha? Enough to push her over?"

"Push over that broad? I don't think so. Jane works out, you know. Ever see the muscles in her arms? She's the kind that works out. No push-over, that one," Martha answered, making it sound like it was a terrible thing for a woman to have muscles. The wrinkled frowns from brow to chin filled her face as her sharp words sounded like a piece of chalk putting dots on a chalkboard.

"Martha? I don't think you're any killer. If I was you, I'd keep all that to yourself until the authorities ask you to answer their questions. Don't offer anything up unless they ask you," I suggested.

"But they'll suspect I'm hiding something, won't they?" she asked.

"They can't suspect what they don't know. Wait it out. They don't even know you talked to her before she keeled over, do they?" I asked.

"No. Guess not. I just can't get the picture out of my head of the ambulance taking her away, though. And to think I caused it."

"Did you see Jane being put into the ambulance?" I asked.

"No. I couldn't look until they closed the doors. I couldn't get the picture out of my head of that woman lying there after I poked her to death," Martha answered.

Her mouth and forehead wrinkled up again in a grimace. Her gaze pierced the dust in my carpet.

"I'm getting an attorney. I don't trust anyone digging into my affairs," Martha added.

"Geez, Martha. If you go and get an attorney before anyone questions you, they'll know for sure you're hiding something. Leave it be," I said.

Martha's put her hands on her temples. "Oh. My head hurts. I'm going home to lie down. She looked back at each of us. "I appreciate all of you listening to me. And this is between us, right? I hear it anywhere else, I'll know where it came from, and there will be hell to pay," Martha said.

I knew she meant it. "You take care of yourself, now, Martha. Rest easy. The truth will come out, somewhere, I said."

"Thanks, Dee." Martha's eyes glazed over. It looked like she was burying her fears and thoughts within herself as she went out the door, shaking her head back and forth.

"Holy cow! Poked her to death! Can you believe that?" I said to Janet and Mary after the door closed.

"Boy. Who'd have thought something like that could have happened? Martha couldn't be the one who did Jane in, do you guys think?" Mary asked.

"Martha talks, well, you know, with definite assertiveness, but I can't see her even scaring Jane," Janet said.

"No. However, something or someone killed Jane and no one has given out any information whether they saw she was shot, or stabbed, or whatever," I said.

"I have my theory, but time will see if that pans out," Mary said.

"And what's that, Mary?" Janet asked.

"Okay. I'll go get the stuff I retrieved and we'll see if there are any clues."

Mary brought in the pictures covered in see-through plastic and the notebook and laid them out on the coffee table.

The third picture gave me a shock.

"Huh. Wow. Would you look at that? Gruesome. Wonder who that is?" I asked.

"Pretty sure this is Jane's ex husband," Mary answered.

"Really! Now look at this set of pictures. Little curly headed kid. Sure is a cutie. Think he's Jane's?"

"Ya. Probably," Mary answered.

"Oh. Here's some of a boy, maybe it's the same one, but older," Janet said.

"Ya. Same curly hair," I added.

"What's all this mean, Mary? What's your theory?"

"Until I read the notebook, I don't want to put anything out there,"

"Now you're holding out. Read the danged thing to us," I said.

Mary looked at the clock on the wall. "Can't right now. I've got to get back home ladies. Sorry, I've gotta go." She gathered up the pictures and the notebook and hurried out the door.

Janet shrugged and got up from the chair and said her 'goodbyes' also. I closed the door behind them, pushing my lips out into a pout, feeling cheated out of some juicy kind of explanation about Jane's former life.

CHAPTER SEVEN

I lay down on my couch, scrunching up the thin pillow under my neck and glanced over at the clock on the wall. I'd forgotten about my Tai Chi class. I hurried to change from sandals to tie-up shoes that better supported my feet before I left.

I drove from the complex to the recreation center where the class takes place and immersed myself in the calming influence of mindful intentions. I pulled in the earth rhythms into my center and pushed out the tainted thoughts of Jane's demise, Martha's confession, and the possibility of evil existing in my surroundings. There were the two men who came to Jane's. How are they involved and what did they hope to find there? Where had all Jane's belongings been taken?

After my return, I started toward the mailboxes and watched as little Margie pushed her cart toward me.

"Hi Margie, how are you today?" I took my time pronouncing my words and talked a bit loud to be sure she understood what I was saying to her.

Margie poked her finger into one ear to adjust the volume on her hearing aid. "I'm pretty well, thank you,

Dee. I have concerns regarding Jane's death. Nobody around here seems to know anything. I must confess, I'm worried that I had something to do with it."

I was astounded.

"Jane lives above me, are you aware of that? Lived, I should say. She often stopped by to see how I am. My advanced age, of course. People wonder when I'll keel over." She laughed and the familiar twinkle in her eyes brightened her face.

"I fixed us each a glass of iced tea. She likes it sweetened, so I put some stevia drops in it. Well, it looked like it was stevia. It is possible I grabbed the liquid Demerol I take for my pain. What if I killed her?"

Margie's wrinkled face turned to an expression of real fear, as her short self peered up at me.

"Oh, Margie, I doubt you made that mistake. Anyway, none of us knows exactly how or why she died."

"What's your opinion? Should I go to the Sheriff and confess?"

"Margie, I think you should go home, take a good look at those two bottles, and try to relive the moment you put sweetener in her tea. Maybe your memory will show you didn't make a mistake and poison her."

"Oh, I do hope so, Dee. I've been worried sick, and with no information coming from anyone, I couldn't help but blame myself." Margie didn't continue speaking and she remained silent for several seconds.

"So, how's your Mother, Dee. I haven't heard you mention her in a long time."

"Thanks for asking. There's been no change in her condition and she seems as happy as you could expect considering her situation."

"Tell me the name of that place? I'm going to put a note on my fridge with that place and phone number in case I go numb some day and can't tell anyone my wishes. My kids are not happy that I'm still living alone."

"It's Pleasant Acres, Margie. I'll get you the contact info. I looked it up on the internet. Their ratings are excellent. Plenty of activities, they have walking paths, and they see to it everybody has an opportunity to get out and stretch their limbs. Of course, it's all with supervision. The food is quite good, too."

"I've ridden by several times, and remembered your Mother lives there. I don't drive anymore, you know. No car, no insurance, no payments. Not such a bad thing. I take taxis where I need to go and look around at stuff I wouldn't see if I was driving, and know what the best thing is? I never have to worry about traffic."

"That's great Margie. Well, I'm on my way to get my mail. I'll get that information to you soon."

We parted and I continued down the sidewalk. The poor dear believes she may have made a mistake. Guess she and Martha share something in common. They're both entertaining the idea they may be responsible for Jane's death. One hated her; the other found her company pleasing.

There was nothing but junk mail in my mailbox. I pushed all of it down into the receptacle provided for throw-aways, but I felt a stiff piece of mail tucked inside. I pulled the advertising sheets back out and found an envelope with my address on it. My address and unit number appeared, but not my name. Mary Elizabeth Burkholder was printed on the envelope. I put the papers back in the bin and decided to take the piece I'd found over to Mary's.

Mary answered the door after I pressed the bell a second time, squinting into the sunlight. "Hi. Come on in. What's going on?"

"You were napping. Sorry I disturbed you."

"S'okay. I needed to get up anyway. What brings you to my door?"

"A piece of mail. It was in my box with my number but has your name."

Mary's sweet-natured cat, a tuxedo breed she named Pepper, wound his way around my ankles. He purred as he gazed up at me.

"He has good taste, Mary, and knows I like cats." I bent over to pet him and gently pulled on his tail, a gesture my cat loves. I handed Mary the item from my mail.

"Hmm. Wonder what this is?" Mary pulled the flap open and began to examine it. Her cheeks turned bright red.

"Bad news?"

"Uh? Oh, no. Umm." She glanced at me and then back at the letter.

"Your cheeks are inflamed."

"It's nothing. Probably a hot flash? You still have those?"

"Ya. Sometimes. I think it's from the blood pressure medication. I'm sure all my hormones took a hike long ago."

"Mine too. I don't take that stuff though."

"Well, something got your engine running."

"Ya. Well, anyway. This is just one of those solicitations for a car dealership. You get those?"

"Yes. More junk. Like I have the means to buy a new car. And don't you look forward to those ads for cremation services?"

"Oh boy. Puts the lively step right back in me." Mary walked into the kitchen and put the letter into her garbage container.

"Sorry I bothered you."

"Lordy. As if we don't get enough advertising. It's twice a week now, have you noticed?"

"Oh! Before I got to the mail boxes, I saw little Margie coming up the sidewalk. Get this. She thinks she may have poisoned Jane by mistake."

"Lordy. Another confession. What was the poison she thought she gave Jane?"

"Liquid Demerol."

"Would have to be quite a bit to kill her. Maybe Jane got high and collapsed. What did you tell her?"

"I told her I thought she should go home and relive her steps; imagine herself fixing the tea and picturing the container she picked up to sweeten the tea. I told her she would realize she hadn't grabbed the wrong container.

"'Course, we don't know that. She may have. Do you suppose we'll ever find out the real cause of Jane's death?"

"I'm thinking because of her stuff disappearing like that, there's some diabolical plot out there we know nothing about."

Mary's cheeks reddened again. "Yes. There is more to it."

"You've read the notebook? Something you wish to share?"

"No, I haven't read it yet, so I don't know anything new. Sorry."

"Your cheeks are red again. You must be guilty of something."

"Lordy. Aren't we all?"

"Mary, me thinks you need to rest, and think about getting an appointment with your doctor. Those cheeks mean something."

"Think so? I'll give it some thought. Bye, Dee. See you later. Pool at six?"

"Yup. I'll be there."

CHAPTER EIGHT

Back at my place, I powered up my computer and began my research. I wondered what is involved when there is a death to investigate. I found a comprehensive Death Investigation Guide. I skimmed through it. There were instructions for how authorities should proceed. Nothing about an investigation by a civilian.

I conclude that no one in this complex has been questioned, or if they were, they are tight lipped about it. Unusual for a group of people who find comfort in discussing in graphic detail all manner of bodily functions. Is it possible they are sworn to secrecy? We witnessed how Jane's residence was cleaned out in a short time, suggesting there is more to learn. Mary is holding back information, I'm sure. Why would she do that?

I turned off the monitor and the computer and decided to rest my eyes and lay back in my lounge chair. I woke with a jerk and looked at the clock on the television console. It was three in the afternoon already. I can't turn on the washing machine until seven in the evening because I have a plan with the power company giving me lower user rates if I wait until then. I thought about vacuuming and doing some dusting, so I set about those tasks. That finished, I fixed a peanut butter sandwich and poured myself a glass of iced tea. Then I washed my face, brushed my teeth and put on my bathing suit and robe. I picked up my sunglasses, rolled my swimming shoes into a large towel, and made my way to the pool.

I stuck my key into the gate and struggled to wiggle the lock open to enter the pool area. Janet and Mary were already in the water when I got there. I wished maintenance had sprayed the lock with lubricant as I'd requested.

"I guess I'm the pool's fool being the last one in, huh?" I shouted.

"Huh? What's a pool's fool? Janet asked.

"I don't know. I made it up. Thought it sounded funny," I answered.

"Pssatt!" Mary said.

"What?" I asked.

"Pssatt!" she repeated.

"What does that mean?" I asked.

"Nothing. Doesn't it sound better than my usual 'lordy'?" Mary asked.

"Oh, I see," I motioned with my fingers forming the letters O, I, C.

"We're a hilarious group tonight!" Janet said.

The three of us began our water exercises, each in our own way.

After several high kicks and waist twists I decided to open up the subject about Jane. "Mary. I've got a few questions for you." I said.

"Ya, what?" she responded.

"Well, I don't understand why you're withholding information from us about Jane. You know stuff we don't and I don't think it's right to keep it from us. Janet and I wouldn't tell anyone what you tell us."

"You're right, Dee. Wait till after we get out of the pool."

"Sounds good to me," I answered.

We finished our half-hour workouts and got out of the pool. When we adjusted our towels on the plastic chairs, each of us sighed and leaned back.

"Well, I'll be quiet so no one overhears our conversation. Keep an eye out for Damon. He's nosy and usually up to no good," Mary explained.

"How do you know that?" I asked.

"Trust me, I know. Anyway, Jane is a complicated person who lived very differently than she did here at Winter Gardens. She never married, but had a long-term relationship with a man of questionable character. She said he treated her well and left her with plenty of money to live on her own. They had a son. That was the curly headed boy you saw in those pictures."

"What about those awful pictures we saw? Looked like someone was pretty bloody." Janet asked.

"I believe that's what's at the crux of her mysterious demise. She told me she witnessed his beating and then his death, but she was sure whoever did it didn't know she was there," Mary said.

"So, she turned them in and now they're after her," I said.

"That makes sense," Janet said.

"Ya. I'm still going through her notes, but some of them are confusing. There are some notes concerning her mother's father. I haven't figured it out yet. I've also tried to find her son. I've had a little success and I've traced him to a California location. Jane gave me the impression she didn't want to be found by her son, but she never told me why," Mary said.

"Did you try those ancestry websites?" I asked.

"Ya, but I can't find her or anyone with any connection to her."

"I bet she changed her name," Janet said.

"That's a possibility," Mary agreed.

"Well, how could you find her son if you're not sure of her former name?" I asked.

"She told me she gave him his father's last name, not hers. There are some murky waters where the father is concerned. I'm not sure where his information could lead me."

"Is this information giving you the red cheeks, Mary?" I asked.

"Oh, I guess that's possible. For some reason, the more I find out, the more scared I get. There are some dark alleys in her life. Not sure if I want to go there."

"Oh gadzooks, Mary. Let me help you dig. Have computer, will investigate." I told her.

"You know how to search on that thing, I don't. Use the names I've found, I guess," Mary answered.

"What can I do to help?" Janet asked.

"Nose around and listen to what people here are saying. Somebody has to know something," Mary suggested.

"Tell you what. I don't believe she's dead, that's what," I said.

"Huh?" Mary said.

"She was whisked away in an ambulance, and so far nobody has been questioned. Her place was cleaned out; what does that add up to?" I said.

"She just fainted or something. Is that what you're guessing?" Janet asked.

"Sure. What else could be going on?" I said.

"And, why is more than one person claiming to have killed her?" Janet asked.

"Guilt. Plain old guilt. Most people didn't like her and they had issues with her." I answered.

"Ya. Remember when we drove up to Hollow Lake in the short bus? The Terminator tried to push her off the cliff," I said.

"Oh, ya. I remember. They got into a shouting match about something and the Terminator gave Jane a shove down the embankment. I had to throw a chain down to help pull her up. You remember, those chains in the back of the bus they use to secure wheelchairs," Janet said. "Only thing I was able find," she added.

"Mary, you and I walked quite a few miles to get to a phone. The darned bus overheated or something. What a day that was!" I said, remembering. "No phone service, and when we got back, everyone was in bad shape because of the heat, even though it wasn't as bad as summer could be.

Afternoon Arizona sun can warm up a car in no time. It was the first time that bunch was quiet for such so long. Nothing but sour faces, once the tow truck got there and got the bus running," I said.

"Now, there's someone else with a motive who might have done something to Jane. And, another thing, why did Jane insist that Mary get things from her apartment if something ever happened to her? Something happened and now you have some sort of information. Oh, boy! What if someone comes looking for what Mary found? Ever think of that?" Janet asked.

I watched Mary's cheeks turn crimson.

"So that's what's going on with you and the red cheeks! Someone *has* contacted you, or warned you about something. Fess up girl," I said.

"No one has contacted me, Dee. I just reacted to your suggestion," Mary answered, her voice soft and pensive.

"You sure?" I asked.

"I appreciate your concern, and I'll take you up on the computer search," Mary said as her voice regained authority.

"Okay. That's a deal. However, we need a strategy meeting," I suggested.

"For what?" Janet asked.

"To strategize, silly. Finding the evidence to show who killed Jane should be simple. If we are able to figure out the motive and the manner of her death, we'd probably come to a conclusion about the killer. Then we book a trip to Belize to hide from him. "It's about the beaches, right?"

Mary and Janet laughed at that suggestion.

And," I paused, "we need a list of questions to be answered and a way to get information. It should include the list of those who have confessed and their reasons. Then we can summarize what we have found out, and what we don't know. How else can we get some proper answers? Do we know who or what authorities we should contact—"

"Or not call at all. After all, no one has come to Winter Gardens asking any questions, have they? That suggests to me something is fishy, out of our control, and more important, the information appears to be out of reach. And who says it's a him? It's possible the killer was a she," Janet said.

"I'm sure there are answers, ladies. We need to be clever in finding what they are," Mary said. "Jane is somehow connected to mob people, because of the father of her son, and there is some old family history her mother suppressed."

"You know that much, huh?" I asked.

"I have reason to believe," Mary answered.

"This is getting juicy," Janet commented. "I say Mary needs to fill us in, we make our lists, divide up what needs to be done, and conquer. Yeah. Conquer. We can do that."

"When does this planning meeting occur?" I asked

"I'll bring over some things for you to look up first, Dee, then, let's meet at my place on Monday after supper. I'd make a meal for you guys but I'm too low on groceries and my social security check isn't due for another week," Mary answered.

"Let's make it pot luck with you opting out," Janet said.

"Sure. That sounds great. Thanks," Mary said. "However, I read in the paper today that pot luck dinners are against the law in Arizona."

"Really," I said.

"The legislature is working on it today, I heard on the news. Maybe they'll change the law. Don't give it another thought," Janet added. "Whew! I'm all heated up from all this conjecture and stuff. Who's coming back with me to the pool?"

Janet and Mary seemed so full of ominous thoughts and surreptitious plans that they descended into the pool with slow and deliberate steps.

My thoughts were on the potluck. I had to decide what to fix and bring. I would love to take a dish, just once, that is better than Janet's. Just once.

CHAPTER NINE

That evening, lightning pierced my bedroom drapes like daggers searching to kill the devil. I tossed and turned until the rumble of thunder joined with the wind and clouds in the distance. Dawn's earliest lights broke out in pieces behind ominous gray billows left over from the rains of the previous night.

The morning news reported that the east valley once again received the brunt of the evening monsoon storm. Downed tree limbs and flooded local streets would impede travel to work for the residents living in those neighborhoods.

I went out early to walk before the sun heated the puddles remaining on the blacktop of the parking lot. I greeted another walker making his way toward me on the sidewalk, his dour looking black pooch straining against his owner's taut leash.

"Hello. Nice morning after last night's rain," I said.

"Hurumph," I heard. "I'm not here to make friends. Move on," he answered.

There are those within these humble dwellings who don't participate in group activities and keep to themselves.

This man is one of them. I've heard whispers about those with pasts who keep hidden from prying eyes and the questions that would follow. Men living alone may be suspect if they are not socially active in the community. Rumors have been sown telling of Chicago underground persons living the last days of their lives in private; former Vatican principals who absconded with ill gotten funds hiding behind plastic vertical blinds, seen late at night walking the paths or using the heated pool. I could write a book.

I'm sure most of it is idle speculation. The man I met could be a widower mad at the world because he is without his house cleaner and caregiver or his lover. I hoped his pooch gives him some comfort and reason for getting up and out each day.

I continued my walk, making my way past the office. A fire engine's siren broke the quiet. The offensive alarm stopped and I walked back around the building and watched as the paramedic/fire truck came through the opened iron gates of our complex. It stopped in front of my building as it does on a frequent basis. The engines continued to run as the men got out of the parked vehicle. An ambulance arrived and the EMT's pushed a gurney into the ground floor alcove toward the elevator.

I observed other early risers walking their dogs, standing next to the animal and then bending over to pick up their leavings to deposit in the blue bags provided by management. Cleaning my cat's box seems easier to me, but that is my preference.

The sun was just beginning to peek out from below the horizon as I made my way back to the front of my building. Mother Nature had hand-painted a perfection of orange and gray clouds laced with blue skies. The palm trees all over the property are swaying because of a slight breeze that helps to cool the air. Those palms don't offer shade to the desert. Their tall trunks rise higher each year seeming to sprout toward the upper atmosphere in an effort to grasp its beauty. I wonder if that is the plan, to not shade the sands because it must be burnt and cleansed and then moved to and fro without spreading disease while it plants wild seeds wherever they come to rest.

As I walked toward the elevator on the ground floor, the doors opened and the EMT's guided a stretcher toward the awaiting ambulance. I stepped aside while the unfortunate woman, who looked pale with her eyes closed against the bright morning sun came out from the alcove. The light seemed to charge suddenly out of the sky as she remained unmoving while the gurney was loaded into the vehicle.

I didn't recognize her, but I felt a stab of sympathy, remembering a similar scene when my mother became ill and needed transportation to the hospital.

I returned home and decided to select something to make for our strategy dinner meeting. I picked up my overflowing folder of recipes. I settled on a Mediterranean hot dish that proved to be an exceptional choice for past suppers, back in Minnesota where I grew up and raised my children. My daughter, who still resides there, asked for the recipe not too long ago, so I know it is a good dish to serve family or company.

I jotted down the ingredients I needed to purchase and stuck the list in my purse, checked for my credit card, sunglasses and car keys. The hour is still early and I shouldn't have to fight for a parking spot close to the grocery store doors.

I soon learned one should never venture out to the local grocery store on the day of advertised specials. You wait until later in the evening, or go another day and forego the specials. During the day, the parking lot fills to capacity. People also come to shop in their golf carts. It can be dangerous for pedestrians to cross the pavement to get into the store because irate shoppers looking for parking spaces tend to get aggressive and too close to those walking. Regularly, a paramedic is called to come to the aid of an unfortunate downed shopper in the parking lot.

You'd think those golf carts would be safe. They can't go as fast as cars, but I learned several years ago, a dapper golfer and his wife were on their way home from the course when he took the corner too fast, and she tipped out of her seat, hit her head on the cement and subsequently died. I read recently that many manufacturers have installed seat belts in the carts.

I walked in the store and pulled out a shopping cart from the group shoved together in an arranged stack and pulled a moistened cloth from the container to wipe off any germs left behind by the last customer. Most elderly people have compromised immune systems and I doubt I am an exception. I selected the items on my list and made my way to the checkout counter. I was second in line; a handsome faced, younger, well-dressed man was in front of me. He turned sideways, pulled his sunglasses down on his nose, and eyed me, frowning. I smiled for no apparent reason. He turned back to his purchases and picked up the single plastic bag filled with his goods. I got a short whiff of his after-shave lotion. He pivoted to look at me again. This time, I frowned, raised my eyebrows, and questioned his gaze. I wondered if I banged the back of his heels with my cart. I doubted it. I'm careful, since I've been the recipient of bashed ankles by careless shoppers on numerous occasions. The young man turned and walked away.

There was an elderly man running the cash register and a woman bagging my groceries who matched his age. I think the store hires these older women more as a way to make the shopping experience positive. She smiles and makes pleasant comments about the weather and how I look as she guides my purchases into the plastic bags. You don't find many stores with paper bags in Arizona because cockroaches love to feed on the glue or the bag, I don't remember which. The cashier inquired if I found everything I was looking for today. I had, and I paid for my purchases with my credit card. I get points for purchases put on my cared and use them to get holiday and birthday gifts. Every penny counts at my age.

At my car, I opened the trunk, put in three plastic bags, and closed it. I had a sense someone was staring at me. A man was looking in my direction from about two rows over. He resembled the man who was in front of me in the checkout line. I had an uncomfortable feeling, gave a shoulder shrug, and got into my car. I rolled down the window, turned on the air conditioner, and waited a minute for the bad air to exit. I turned my eyes to gaze where I saw the man, and he was no longer visible. I drove out of the parking lot without another encounter.

I checked my rearview mirror several times on my way back to Winter Gardens, but there was no sign of anyone following me. Those concerns vanished as I put my groceries away, cleaned the cat box, and prepared my garbage for the daily pick up.

The mix of ground veal and pork, spices, noodles and a cream sauce with melted cheese smelled mighty good as I prepared the hot dish I selected to bring.

Around five in the evening, I gathered up some towels and wrapped up the glass baking dish filled with the heated hot dish I prepared and headed over to Mary's.

We greeted each other with enthusiastic greetings and deposited our homemade goods on Mary's kitchen counter.

"Wow. What wonderful smells you guys brought to my kitchen. This is great," Mary said.

"Janet, what did you bring? It smells wonderful!" I asked.

"Veal scaloppini. Hope you like it," Janet answered.

"Guess that trumps my hot dish, yet again," I remarked.

Mary provided iced tea and fresh rolls and we sat at her dining table enjoying every morsel of food.

"Somebody was taken to the hospital early this morning from my building," I said.

"Who?" Janet asked.

"No one I know. Maybe someone will know who if we go to coffee tomorrow," I suggested. "And, I had a small incident at the grocery store this morning. A young man kept looking at me when I was in line to pay for my stuff. I saw him again looking my way in the parking lot," I told them.

"I bet he thought you're cute and wanted to make contact. What'd he look like?" Mary asked.

"Ordinary," I answered. "Nothing remarkable."

We finished the meal and shoved all the dishes into the dishwasher after rinsing them. Apartment dishwashers are notorious for not being the best at getting dishes clean, and these appliances were no exception.

We moved to the living room and perched in our favorite chairs. Mary liked her recliner, Janet chose the straight-backed chair, and I preferred the couch.

The coffee table had three small stacks of paper with a notebook under each stack.

"I put little things together for each of us and gave you a notebook for you to keep track of what you've done and what you've found out," Mary explained.

"Very efficient," I commented.

"It's not a lot at this point, but the information we gather will be helpful," Mary said.

Mary handed out the small piles.

I looked at my list. It contained items I would research on the Internet. There was a small photo tucked inside the notebook. I turned it over. It was a picture of a young man, taken from a distance, dressed in a suit standing next to a building in the downtown of what seemed to be a large city. I blinked and drew in my breath. I was looking at the same person I'd seen at the grocery store.

"Uh, guys, take a look at this," I said, holding the picture up for them. "Mary, who is this?"

"Could be Jane's grown son, but I'm not positive," she answered.

"I think this looks like the fella that was in front of me at the grocery store," I said.

"Your imagination is running overtime, Dee. My latest information shows that he lives and works in New York City,"

"Really," I said. "Whoever it was reminded me of someone. I still think it could have been Jane's son."

"I'm going to enjoy getting the information you want, Mary. I'm going to go to all the game nights, all the coffee times and go on the bus trips. I always tune in my ears to gossip. I bet I'm going to find out lots of juicy stuff. I bet Manny would be a good source." Janet said.

"Huh? Oh. Manny. Sure," Mary answered. "You're going to have to figure out a way to get people to tell you things, too, Janet. Someone must have seen and heard things when Jane died. Little bits of information could get us the answers we're looking for," Mary said.

"Now, what are you working on, Mary?"

"I'm still figuring out Jane's lineage. Her notebook has pictures and references to ancestors from Europe. Jane told me her mother was adamant about never discussing her family or where they came from. Why, I don't know," Mary said.

"You've also told us that Jane's umm, well, the father of her son, was of dubious character. What about that bloody picture? Was that him?" I asked.

"Ya. He was, 'connected', I believe the word is," Mary said.

"Yuk. Those kinds of people give me the creeps," I said. "You should be careful who you contact regarding that man."

"I'm not contacting anyone at this point," Mary said.

"They contacting you?" Janet asked.

"No. I've received odd phone calls though. Hang ups. Heavy breathing, that sort of thing," Mary said.

"Oh dear. Either a pervert or—" I said.

"Hard to tell. I received pieces of mail too," Mary said.

"For real? Like what?" I asked.

"One letter sent to me just had the words 'Consider This A Warning' printed in large red letters, Mary answered.

"What? Why didn't you tell us you were being threatened?" I asked.

"I got caught up in going to the post office to report and document it, and then I guess I thought that would take care of it," Mary answered.

"Don't think so," Janet said.

"Well, I took it to the main post office in Daystar City. They told me it was mailed from the downtown post office facility. They told me to fill out some forms so there would be a record of it if I receive any more," Mary explained.

"That is downright scary. You said 'some pieces of mail', Mary. What else did you get?" Janet asked.

"There was a note shoved under my door one day. It said the same thing," Mary answered.

"So twice now!" I said. "This is serious."

"I've been paying close attention when I go anywhere now. So far, I haven't noticed anyone following me," Mary said.

"Mary, I don't think you are taking this seriously enough. You need protection. Aren't you scared?"

"I bought a can of pepper spray. I keep it in my pocket, and my cell phone too," Mary said.

"Your phone turned on?" I asked.

"Ya." Mary answered.

"That's not enough. It's no help at all if someone sneaks up behind and conks you on the head," Janet said. "Listen you guys, something very bad is going on. All of us need to be watchful and, you know what? I think we should call the Sheriff about this. Someone is targeting Mary and they need to know about it."

"Will you call them, Janet?" Mary asked.

"How about I come to your place and be with you when you call them," she suggested.

"Alright. Tomorrow?" Mary asked.

"Yes. I'll be there at 10:00 AM."

"Okay," Mary said.

"Listen. How about you quit going anywhere by yourself. There's safety in numbers you know," I said.

"Okay. I'll call one of you when I go out. We could go grocery shopping together and things like that," Mary answered.

"Please don't get sick. I can't stand waiting in doctor's offices," Janet said.

"Pssaat! I don't get sick," Mary answered.

I yawned. It was well past the time I get into my lounge chair to watch TV.

"Ya, I should go, too, Mary. This has been an evening to remember. Good food, pretty scary stuff you have going on, and I've got my gossiping to get to. Coffee tomorrow?" Janet asked. "After we call the Sheriff?"

"I suppose. Nothing like a stimulating bodily functions gone wrong review to get my mind off of this stuff," Mary said.

Janet and I left together.

"It seems like Mary is dismissing those threats too easily. What do you think?" I asked.

"I agree, but at least the authorities will know about it tomorrow, in case something else happens," Janet said.

"I think we need to keep prodding her, or we'll never find out if anything else happens," I said.

"Yup, she has a tendency to keep things to herself," Janet said. "I'm really afraid to think what those threats could mean. We're together a lot, too. We could be next, ya know."

"Now that you mention it, maybe so. Especially after I saw that man watching me in the parking lot. Gives me the creeps," I said.

"We need to stay more aware of our surroundings, don't you think?" Janet asked.

"Definitely," I answered.

We walked together without conversation until we reached the divide in the sidewalks.

"Do you think anyone missed us at the pool tonight?" Janet asked.

"Damon might miss us," I answered.

"Who?" she asked.

"You know, the guy who sits out on his patio and oogles the ladies swimming in the pool," I answered.

"Oh ya. Well, see you in the morning. Sleep tight," Janet said as she headed toward home. "Keep those boogey men out of your dreams," she added.

"You too!"

CHAPTER TEN

The next day I got out of bed earlier than my usual six AM. I make it a practice in the morning to be dressed and presentable as early as I can manage. I turned on my lighted mirror and focused on my wrinkles while I made up my brows, cheeks, and lips to look as perky and unold as possible. You never know what might happen and then you are caught looking like the elderly person you are, or as if you'd been dragged from a nap or slumber without warning.

I had signed up for the bus tour of Daystar City and I arrived at the Clubhouse on time.

"Thought you guys were gonna call the Sheriff today," when I saw Mary and Janet waiting outside the clubhouse.

"Forgot I'd signed up for this," Mary answered.

"Me too. Oh well," Janet added. "We didn't know you were going, either," Janet said.

Mary sat with Janet and I sat with Manny, Jane's rumored paramour.

The bus jerked and groaned as it maneuvered around the corner and out of the complex.

"I miss her, Dee. I really miss her," Manny said.

"Who?"

"Jane, of course," he answered.

"No, I don't know, Manny. I have heard rumors, but I don't believe all of them," I said.

"I feel so responsible," he said.

"Responsible for what?" I asked.

"Her death."

"What? How can that be?"

Manny leaned closer to me. That wasn't a big move since the seats are less than generous. He did put his lips close to my ear.

"I think I, uh, contributed to her death."

"Manny!"

"Shhh. I'm not proud of what I did."

"What did you do?"

The bus stopped at our destination at that moment. Manny wore an expression indicating to me that he would continue this disturbing conversation another time.

I said, "When?'

He mouthed the answer, "Later."

Oh geez. Now Manny thinks he had something to do with Jane's death! I hurried over to where Janet and Mary were standing waiting for me.

"You guys won't believe what Manny just said to me!" I said.

"Let me guess," Janet said. "He wants to leave his wife for you."

"Oh! Can you imagine?" I asked.

"Well, what did he say?" Mary asked.

Our conversation was interrupted when a tall, well-dressed senior citizen stepped out of the building where our tour bus would take us around Daystar City.

"Excuse me. May I have your attention, please?" he asked.

At least twenty-four people were also waiting to go on the tour and they all turned to listen.

"I'm sorry to tell you our bus has broken down. We have arranged for several SUV's to take you on the tour. The drivers are volunteers from our community and know the history of our wonderful city. Now, if you will divide up we'll get you on your way."

Our driver was short, wore a ball cap and white sneakers. He didn't crack a smile or say a word when we piled in the back seat and he didn't offer his name.

Janet raised her eyebrows while pointing to the driver. I imitated her expression with mine in the 'I don't know' position. Mary smiled at us and then she spoke.

"Hi. I'm Mary and these are my friends Janet and Dee."

Our driver issued a grunt, and then turned on the ignition. We drove a short wordless time until he pulled up in front of a small cement brick home.

"This here's the museum. Go in and they'll tell you about it," our driver stated.

"Okee, dokey, then," I said, raising my eyebrows in the 'we know how well educated this dude is' position.

We spent at least forty-five minutes with a woman who told us about how Daystar City began. The house is a well-preserved original structure reflecting the era of the people who first populated the city. I left the group to go into a bedroom where I found a wall covered with pictures and information about the man whose idea it was to build a community for persons fifty-five and older and to operate the recreation centers with volunteers. A man of vision and intelligence, far ahead of his time, he and his crew built several model homes in the first months of 1960, advertised the joys of retiring to Arizona and were shocked to have some 500 visitors the first day of showings.

It was tough to get a good view of the small house and there was little room to navigate. I was determined get a peek into each room and managed to wriggle through the crowd of people with countless 'excuse me's'.

The three of us walked outside when the house tour finished and we sighed together and looked for our transportation to other areas of the city.

A tall individual made his way toward us.

"Ladies? I believe you are the women I need to take on the rest of the tour. Follow me," he said.

"What happened to Chatty Charles?" I asked.

"Who?" he asked.

"Sorry. Our other driver," I said.

"He's sick and called for a substitute," he explained.

I couldn't place his accent. Sounded like somewhere between a farm and New York City.

The substitute driver was no more talkative than the first. In fact, he looked like someone right out of a mobster movie. His hair was dyed a dark color, slicked back into a modified ducktail, his mustache was stiff and shaped into long thin spears pointing up onto his cheeks. Even the car fit the character. It was a remarkable gangster car, restored with suicide doors, tan and black in color, white walled tires, and shined to perfection.

"Beautiful car you have here," I commented.

Wouldn't you know it? He pulls out a big fat cigar and lights it in the car, takes a few puffs and says, "Tanks."

The three of us coughed and then he rolled down the driver's side window.

We were supposed to be going around all of Daystar City and visiting each of the recreation centers, but the driver seemed to be using other streets to go somewhere else.

"Hey. This isn't where were supposed to be going," I said.

He laughed a hoarse guttural sound. "Never mind girlies. I'm taking you somewhere I bet you've never been. You're going to love it," he answered.

I gave the heave ho sign to Janet and Mary as we pulled up to a stop sign. We flew out of the doors that opened the opposite of where doors open in modern day automobiles.

"Run!" I yelled. I grabbed Mary's hand. She can't run much because of the arthritis in her feet so I had to help her.

The driver shouted at us as we ran. "Come back here! You're gonna—" his words were hard to hear as we focused on retreat. We locked arms to help each other move as fast as possible from the threat and headed for one of the houses. My thought was to get through one of the home's gates and hide in their backyard.

We heard the car's engine roar, then the sound of the brakes grinding the vehicle to a stop followed by a dog's yelp.

We managed to get up one of the driveways next to a house. I opened the latch on the fence gate and we rushed in. I peeked through the slats.

"What's going on?" Janet asked.

"I think he hit a dog. Oh, someone is out there. He just picked up the dog. Doesn't look like the dog was hurt. Now he's talking to the driver."

I turned to Mary and Janet. "You guys okay? We kinda dragged each other."

"Ya, I'm okay. I kinda scraped the side of my foot though," Mary said.

Janet bent over to look at Mary's foot. "It's not bleeding, but you're shaking, Mary."

"I'm scared, that's all," she replied.

"Me, too," I said. "But we'll be able to leave as soon as that guy gets the hell out of here."

Janet joined me at the fence. "They're still talking, looks like. Oh, the man with the dog stepped back and now the car is leaving. Let's stay here until we're sure he doesn't circle back."

We waited fifteen minutes. No cars drove by. I hoped we had lost him or he'd given up.

I peered through the slats again. I didn't see anyone or the car.

"Let's get out of here," I told Janet and Mary.

Janet helped Mary up onto her feet.

We walked toward the gate, opening it with care, taking time to survey the area to avoid any surprises.

"I think we were lucky no one at this house has noticed we are here," Mary commented.

"We were also danged lucky he didn't come back, to look for us," I said.

Janet closed the gate without a sound and we stopped to get a look around us when we reached the sidewalk.

"For safety's sake, let's walk further into this neighborhood. If he comes back we can go to another house," Janet suggested.

Two blocks down the street we walked smack dab into a nice little park. A canopy of various trees, Palo Verde, Acacia and a few Ironwoods formed an arch, bending into one another as if to shelter walkers, as well as grasses and small animals from sun and storms. Talk about luck! The sweat was pouring down our foreheads as we headed for the restroom located at the far end of the park. I looked behind us as we ducked in. Nobody following, and no sign of the car. I didn't see another person in the area either. Too hot for kids and parents to be out playing.

Lucky for us there was cool water coming out of the bathroom faucets. I stood watch while Janet and Mary freshened up.

"Got your cell phone, Dee?" Mary asked, her breath coming in gasps.

"Yup. Kids tell me to never leave home without it," I answered.

"Call a cab. I'll pay for it," Janet said.

"Where the hell are we? I can't ask to be picked up if I don't know where we are," I said.

"Turn on your GPS. That'll tell you where we are," Janet said.

"Ya. Right. Like I know how to do that," I answered.

"Gimme it. I'll figure it out," Janet said as she grabbed my phone.

"Here. We're here. Northern Daystar City. Tell this to the cab company," Janet instructed, pointing to the map on my phone.

"Good plan." I dialed the preprogrammed number of my favorite cab company and made the request for a pick up. Then I took my turn at the sink, patting the wetness into my skin and letting it drip all over me. I put a scoop in my hand and placed it on the back of my neck. I felt instant relief. I looked up at myself in the mirror. Those were some red cheeks looming back out at me.

"Cab should be here any minute, girls," I said.

"Not a second too soon. I'm wiped. My heart is popping out of my chest," Mary said.

"Mary. Inhale deep and let it out slow. Can't have you going horizontal on us. What the hell was that about, do you suppose?" Janet asked.

"Where was he planning on taking us?" I asked.

"Why did he take us somewhere besides where we were supposed to go?" Janet asked.

"One of Mary's weird friends. Gotta be. Nothing like this ever happens to us, does it?" I asked.

"Oh, come on. We don't know what that ding-dong had going on. I am going to report it, though," Mary said.

"For sure!" Janet and I said in unison.

"You okay now, Mary?" I asked.

"My feet are killing me, but I'll survive," she answered.

"Janet, you booked out there. Keeping in shape, are we?" I asked

"I try," she answered.

We watched with relief as the green cab pulled up by the restrooms.

"Don't get in until you see his face," I suggested. "We don't know if that creep sent us someone from his legions of no-gooders."

The cabbie got out of the car. He looked innocent enough and I nodded my head in approval.

The ride back to Winter Gardens was a treat with cold air conditioning blowing hard giving us relief from overheating. Each of us began to feel better by the time we came through the gates.

Janet paid the driver. We stood on the sidewalk for a moment, looking at each other.

"Now, that's an experience I don't want to repeat anytime soon," I said.

"It's too hot to stand here. Let's talk about it later," Janet said.

"You should call the tour company though, Janet. They need to know about that wacko, I said.

"Okay. I'll do that," she answered.

We said our goodbyes.

CHAPTER ELEVEN

I made it to my rental, but not without stumbling when a small rock on the sidewalk found its way under my shoe. I was exhausted and not in complete control of where my legs and feet were taking me. The heat and running had taken its toll.

My phone rang immediately as the door closed behind me. I looked at the caller ID. It was the Nursing home where Mom is staying. I always fear the worst and my heart thumped hard as I answered.

The caller's words rang in my ear over and over. 'I'm very sorry, Dee, but your mother passed as she napped this afternoon. It was peaceful with no pain or anxiety.'

I absorbed her words, 'I'm very sorry.' Oh crap. This is the worst way to end a day. The absolute worst. Never mind what happened earlier. That was a piece of key lime pie compared to this.

"I'll be right there."

That dear sweet woman, my mother, lay on her lace-embellished pillowcase, the one I brought as a gift on Mother's Day. It was not regulation or within their rules, but at her age, they let it pass. She was pale and lifeless.

She looks different now from when she was alive with no memory. There is a grayish pallor about her face and her lips are dark and seem to have a touch of maroon on them. Or is it bluish. I'm staring at her in disbelief. I pulled up a chair next to her bed, took a cool hand in mine, and sat for a long while, letting the sadness take hold. I find the end of life puzzling. Even though our love could no longer be shared as it once was, all the years of stored-up memories flooded through my brain, seeming to help ignore her actual death for a moment. Is this how I am to grieve? Reliving past experiences that become deposited into some storage bank where eventually they will fade and die? Is that the true end of life? When memory can no longer be recalled or there is no one left to remember?

Ugh. I am sad beyond my own believing. So what, she had a long, long life? It is never long enough. I am angry and aware my own life won't go on long enough to suit me. I'm mad she's been taken from me. Furious at my own mortality. Selfish, huh? Poor dear didn't know who I was at the end, but that didn't stop me or anyone else from caring. I won't lose memory of her, and my children won't either. What did she leave behind that could prompt remembrances of her decades from now? For that matter, what will I leave behind?

114

My head fell to my chest as I continued to hold her hand. My almost silent sobs sounded like squelched hiccups. My breaths came in distorted gulps as tears began to drip on my lap. I am embarrassed to allow my emotions to be seen or heard.

I wasn't aware the nurse had stepped into the room and was standing beside me until I heard her heavy sigh. I turned my face and looked into the countenance of a woman I knew had seen this before, yet had the grace and training to offer comfort. I took the tissue from her hand and blew my nose hard. She laid her hand gently on my shoulder. It seemed to release some of my pain. She asked me to come with her when I was ready. I'll never be ready, but it must be done. I picked up the music box off the table and followed without speaking, into a small room where there were papers to fill out, and questions to answer.

The staff was helpful and made the tasks easier. I let them know I would be in contact as soon as a memorial date was set. It was time for me to exit these doors for the last time as a visitor. I couldn't bear to look at anyone, or the walls or the floor. My feet felt like they were loaded with lead and if my head was any heavier, I would topple over. I had a vision of myself going down, plop, then right back up, and plop down again. I laughed at myself. A stupid vision to relieve the stress. It was then I thought today should have been cancelled due to lack of interest.

The nurse who walked with me to the exit doors made a queer remark.

"Take care of yourself, Dee. You look a sight. Take time to put yourself in order," she said.

I looked in the rearview mirror when I got into my car. *Oh, my. No wonder she said that. I should have cleaned myself up a bit before I came. She must think I've lost my marbles.*

I called Mary and Janet as soon as I arrived home. They visited my mother several times while she was alive and gave her the ballet dancer music box. I put it on the table next to me, fiddling with the girl's dainty shoes as we discussed dates and times.

We decided on a day to have a memorial after I cleared the date with my children and friends. I called the home and requested the small room for such occasions for a few hours in the afternoon the following Friday. Next, I called my children to confirm their arrival.

My Mother requested her remains be donated for science so all I needed to do was call the business to arrange it. Simple. Just like that. Poof, you're gone.

However, not gone from all those corners and masses of brain matter in my head.

"You need to cool off and get some rest, Dee," Mary suggested when I called her back.

"I haven't eaten yet. Let me put a sandwich together and I'll meet you at the pool," I said.

"I'll tell Janet, okay?" Mary said.

I fixed a bologna sandwich, ate a container of applesauce, poured a cold glass of water, emptied it, and went on my way.

I peered through the iron gate at the pool. Manny was there, chatting up a storm with Mary. Looked like he was whispering in her ear. They stopped talking and jumped into the water in one simultaneous motion.

Janet reached the gate when I did and she opened it for me. We put our towels on the chairs and stepped in the pool with a collective 'ahhh'.

I'm not sure what I would do without these friends and the comforting coolness the pool offers. I'm never sorry I chose this place to live with the benefit of a pool 24/7. The soothing water does more than calm my body; it also clears my head of cobwebs, the kind that hold dark thoughts, sadness, and confusion.

Manny turned in the water to speak to me. "You had a bad day, Dee. I'm sorry to hear about your mother," he said.

His wavy white hair glistened when the nighttime pool lights came on. He shook the water from his head and continued. "Whoever that bozo is that took you guys for a ride is going to pay for it. We're going to find him and do, well, something," he said.

"I called the Heritage Center and complained about the driver, and I told them what happened to us," Janet said.

"Which was not a heck of a lot," I added. "We don't even know for sure where we were!"

"I think I do," Manny said. "There's a neighborhood I'm familiar with in northern Daystar City I think might be it. I will take Mary there and we'll see if that's where you ended up. I already talked to her about it."

"What is it going to prove, finding out where we were?" I asked.

"Seems like a dead zone to me. What's the point of finding it?" Janet asked.

"Something forgotten will be remembered," Manny offered.

I couldn't concentrate on anything more so I turned and side stroked my way to the far end of the pool. I stayed there for several minutes facing away from them and letting the tears roll down my cheeks.

I wiped my face with the back of my hand and looked up at the sky. Clouds were building to the east and I saw a flash of lightning.

"Storm coming you guys. We better get out of here," I said.

Janet and Mary disappeared but Manny hung back.

"I didn't get a chance to explain," Manny said.

"You know, Manny, I'm pretty disgusted with you right now. The rumors in this place concerning your womanizing are sickening. Barbara deserves better from you."

"It's not what it looks like Dee. Let me explain," Manny answered.

The palm trees began bending down as the wind blew hard and the sky turned yellowish beige, threatening to dump the contents of the billowing clouds down on us.

"Not now Manny. I'm going home."

CHAPTER TWELVE

Friday came faster than I'd anticipated. The airport shuttle brought my children to my complex. They put their bags in the living room and pulled me close in a giant three-way hug. I held on for several moments.

"Anything you want me to do?" my oldest, Jennifer, asked.

"Oh, it's so good to have you here," I said. "Guess you could put your bags in the bedroom. I have a couple of racks put out for them."

"Nice portable bed you have in there, Mom," Brian commented.

"I'll take that one, Jen, you take my bed, and Brian, you can have the hide-a-bed. I know that's comfy because I slept on it after I bought it," I said.

"You look tired, Mom. Did you get any decent rest this week?" Brian asked.

"Some. There's been some upsetting things going on, none of your concern, of course, and I'm sure knowing your Grandma is gone forever added to my stress," I answered.

"Wish we could have visited her more," Jennifer said.

"She wouldn't have remembered who you are. Once in a while she recognized me," I explained.

"What were the upsetting things, Mom?" Brian asked

"I think we, meaning, Janet, Mary and myself, have it fairly well taken care of. Did I tell you about the death of one of our residents?" I asked.

"You told me, Mom. I don't know if you shared the information with Brian," Jennifer said.

"No, you didn't. Don't resident die fairly regularly here?" Brian asked.

"Yes, but this one was different," I said.

I explained Jane's demise, leaving out the threats and the driver who tried to take us to an unknown destination.

"All the confessions and how they thought they killed her are plausible, but you won't know the true story until you find out how she actually died," Brian commented.

"Exactly. Now, where do you want to have dinner?" I asked.

"Mexican, Mom. Know a good authentic restaurant?"

"I sure do. No reservation needed," I answered.

* * *

Since this was their first visit, the next day I did the obligatory tour of my space and then we walked around the buildings and grounds.

"Mom. Do you ever use these grills? They're nice."

"Huh?"

"That's the second question I've asked you and you don't answer. Are you okay?" Jennifer asked.

"Sorry. Can't stop thinking about my Mom and the memorial."

Jennifer took my arm and pulled me close to her.

While we were in the clubhouse, Brian and Jennifer roamed around the rooms and I happened to overhear Ron talking to the maintenance man. Neither were aware I was within hearing distance of their conversation. It was then I remembered Ron telling the him there were no files in his desk with information regarding Jane, her apartment, or anything pertaining to her. Ron sounded distressed, as if he'd looked for files, but found none. I mulled this over in my mind, and missed another question from one of my children.

"Oh. Sorry. I was in la-la land for a minute. What was it you asked?" I said.

"I'm curious about the organ recital note on the bulletin board, is all, Mom."

"Oh that. Don't know who put it there. Some folks believe we want to hear all the gory details of their latest surgery or ailments and the note is trying to discourage those conversations."

They laughed in unison.

My children are adults, have supported me in each move and change I've made in my life, and we find it easy to be together even if there is little conversation. They have turned into nice people and they make me feel important in their lives even though we are living in different states.

We finished the tour of the complex and went back to my apartment to freshen up before we left for the memorial. I drove to the care facility with my family in tow. Janet followed in Mary's car. We parked and all walked to the entrance together. The manager of Pleasant Acres met us at the door and escorted us into the small room meant for private meetings or events.

I set a box on a side table and began to remove its contents. I had several pictures of my mother at various stages of her life and one when she turned 90. I set the music box on the table after I wound it up. All of us sat without talking while the sweet tune tinkled, breaking the silence.

I turned and faced the small gathering and was surprised to see the manager had stayed and Mother's favorite nurse had joined us as well. There were eight or ten residents escorted by aides, smiling with sympathy. I assumed they remembered my mother even if she never mentioned them. I smiled, although it wasn't strong enough to cover the emotions causing my lips to tremble. I looked up from my notes and realized Manny and his wife Barbara were there also. I realized then there's more than one side to him. I am happy they decided to attend.

I read from my prepared text, a list of highlights in my Mother's life. I told them about her struggles and successes. I wanted my children to realize how much I admired her independence. She was married, had a college degree, yet spent her childbearing years at home becoming a great housekeeper, wife, and mother. She maintained memberships in several academic groups, studied religious concepts to decide what fit best in her life, was a voracious reader, and supported her husband in his endeavors in business. I saw by the expressions on my children's faces that they were not aware of all I'd said. Mother believed in her children's abilities whether limited or great and was a constant cheerleader for their efforts. I only hoped that I'd learned to emulate her and to carry on the familial support of my offspring.

Once again, I wound up the ballerina. The small gathering of those who meant the most to my mother listened with smiles beginning to creep across their faces. One by one, Mary, Janet, Mother's nurse, the manager, even Barbara and Manny, began to waltz about the room with me, the aides wheeled their occupants around in rhythm with the tune, our smiles turning to laughter as my children joined in the dance. It was a fitting tribute to a fine woman who brought joy and love to all she met.

CHAPTER THIRTEEN

Jennifer and Brian stayed on a few days after my Mother's memorial. Jennifer shopped for groceries, filling my freezer with salmon and steaks I seldom purchase because of their high prices. I found a couple of nice bottles of wine she'd put in the cupboard and cheeses and crackers I could have on hand for my friends.

Brian fixed the table lamp that had been teetering precariously on the table for several weeks awaiting attention. He vacuumed the bedrooms and the living room, which sent shockwaves through my bones, since I'd never seen him do anything like that while growing up. He exchanged all my light bulbs with LED bulbs, claiming I should find a difference in my electric bill.

"Anything else you need or want?" They both asked.

"A tall, dark and handsome man would be nice, but that's kinda out of your abilities to provide, I believe," I answered.

"Is it hard, living alone, Mom?" Jennifer asked.

"Yes and no. I like having my own space, but night after night without discussion of big or little things is hard.

And I've noticed, from comments from other residents, that once they've reached their eighties, several doctors have been known to tell them there is nothing more they can do for them. I don't understand that. We've reached advanced years, contributed to society, mostly for the good of all, and continue to look after one another in our old age. Now, babies, on the other hand seem to be considered far more important. The medical communities bend over backwards to keep premature and sick babies alive with every available procedure," I said.

"If any doctor of yours comes up with that 'nothing more we can do' statement, I want to know about it," Brian said.

"Ditto," Jennifer added.

"Of course. I'm off my soapbox now," I said.

We went out to dinner one more time. They chose a restaurant known for their outstanding burgers, something I seldom eat.

***

Once my children returned to their respective homes and my heart began to heal, my conversations with my friends returned to discussions about our everyday lives and the mystery of Jane's death.

Janet fulfilled her task of going to coffee as often as possible to gain some insight into what residents might know or speculate. She was eager to relay her conversations with us Friday night at the pool.

"Did you get any information from anyone?" Mary asked.

"Yes, and no," Janet replied. "Get this. Pristine Christine, you remember, the new gal with brassy blonde hair, she's the one who wears the expensive clothes and always looks perfect."

"Like you?" I asked.

"Maybe. However, she wears her outfits with attitude, superior like. I complimented her on her new sandals, cuz they're similar to mine. She said, 'they're from Neiman Marcus, of course,' as if I couldn't afford to shop there. Oh ya, I said, I'm familiar with that store, Needless Markup. I don't think she liked my humor." Janet laughed at her joke.

"Hah! Better than 'Fart and Smile', 'Came Apart' or 'Booger Fling,' I said.

"She'd had a fit if I'd suggested she goes to those places," Janet said.

"What's 'Fart and Smile and "Booger Fling'?" Mary asked.

"Oh. Don't you know?" That's Smart and Final, a discount store, K Mart, and Burger King." Janet explained. "Teenage humor."

"Okay for that. But, come on. Did you ask any dig up dirt questions?" Mary asked.

"Didn't need to. The whole group was abuzz about Damon. Guess he's invited several of the women here to his place after late evening swims. Tells them he takes the 'little blue pill' and welcomes them to go to his apartment for a sleepover," Janet explained.

"Wait a minute here," I said. "His wife wouldn't allow that."

"Rumor is, she went out of town a while ago to be with her dying brother," Janet said.

"Pssaat!" Mary said. "The rat will play while the swan is away. What a creep."

"I heard he's been window peeping too. Somebody complained and Damon is on notice to clean up his act or management will force him to vacate. I bet the manager needs proof, first though," Janet said.

"Can you imagine?" I said. "Who'd want to be the one taking pictures of that?"

Group giggles. Mary broke the mild hilarity

"You still didn't get any new information about Jane," Mary complained.

"You haven't been forthcoming with information, either, Mary. What did you read in the notebook you found?" I asked.

Mary stopped to look at me. Her expression was somber, almost a glare.

"I haven't turned up anything that seemed worth sharing, that's all," she explained.

"Oh. Well, Janet, go on with what you were going to say," I said.

"Damon was at coffee one of those mornings and he's claiming he saw some guy, late at night, going to the elevator and coming back out with Jane on his arm. The next day, they found Jane downed on the second floor."

"Manny says Damon was sure it was Jane's son. Now, how is that possible?" Janet asked. "How does he even know she has one?"

"I don't have a clue," Mary answered. "I think Manny is incorrect in his conclusion. Jane told me she hasn't had contact with her son. Something is fishy here."

I had ideas of my own. "How about this? I've noticed, for the last couple of months, a piece of equipment attached to the guardhouse at the front gate that looks like a security camera. Maybe we take it down some night and find out if it has recorded anything that could give us some answers. Like, who was with Jane that night."

"You've got to be kidding," Mary said. "First of all, how do we get it off there without serious personal injury, second, not get caught, third, who's got a ladder to get up there and the equipment to view what's on there. That's just some of my concerns."

"Are we sure it is a camera?" Janet asked.

"I think I heard Manny tell me a while back that Management was going to install one. Bet they did," I offered.

"And we all realize how reliable Manny's information is," Mary commented.

"Some of what he says turns out to be true. The law of probability," I offered.

"You're the most friendly with Manny," Janet suggested to me. "You can ask him to help."

I was reluctant to agree. I am only sort of acquainted with Manny and for some reason unknown to me, he confides things to me without my solicitation.

"Oh, I almost forgot. Tilly has had more sightings of the man in the palm tree," Janet said.

"Really. What now?"

"She described how he has made some of the dead palm leaves into a makeshift chair. Apparently, he swings in it," Janet said.

"Huh. That is bizarre. Could that really happen?" I asked.

"Tilly says she is upset that we don't believe her, so she's going to call the Sheriff and ask them to join her on her patio one night so that she can verify her sightings. She is sincere about this," Janet said.

"I hope Tilly hasn't developed an eyesight problem or something mentally going askew," Mary said.

"I believe she definitely sees something up there, but what exactly, I can't say," I said.

"Hope she finds someone who sees what she thinks is there," Janet said. She stood up and turned to the both of us. "I've got to get going. I'm quite tired. See you all later." She yawned and went out the gate.

Mary and I picked up our towels, put on our bathing suit cover-ups and exited out the gate together.

***

I was able to ask Manny about the camera removal a day or so after the girls suggested it. I saw him at the mailboxes and walked with him for a while.

"Manny, is it true that a surveillance camera was installed on the guard house?"

"Ya. Ron told me they were going to get one. There's been complaints about unauthorized people getting in here. Why do you want to know?"

"Well, Damon told people at coffee that he saw someone coming out of the east elevator with Jane the night before she died. I'd like to get hold of some footage and see who it was," I answered.

"Hmm. Well, how are you going to do that?" he asked.

"I hoped you would help," I said.

"Let me get back to you on that," Manny said. The sharp tone of his voice indicated I surprised him with my request.

At this point, I speculated about Damon. I think he's a creep. I seldom conversed with him but I had observed him speaking with others. He used exaggerated hand movements. Does that distract the listener so he can easily lie? Manny talked to him more than me. If rumors were true about his philandering with other women, maybe he was the last person with Jane before she died.

Weeks passed and I did not hear from Manny about dismantling the camera. In the meantime, I spent my time taking care of my mother's things. I donated the items still usable and shipped a small chest of drawers to my son and a hand-crocheted bedspread to my daughter. Other more personal things had been distributed when she first took up residency at the extended care facility.

Janet, Mary, and I went shopping together, after our decision Mary should not go out alone. We arrived at the nearby grocery store, our coupons clutched in our hands and our resolve to shop the bargains intact. The store was crowded and the din of chatter high enough to send the derelict birds to the tops of the rafters to hide. We swabbed down our carts with the sanitizing wipes provided at the entrance and set off in separate directions, promising to meet close to the exit in one hour.

I made my way to the meat counter and met another fellow resident. I would describe her as a gadfly. Kathleen has a dour personality but her taste in clothing is far from it. Today her light brown hair was streaked with red and orange and her billowy dress was hot pink and red mixed together. She is not a small person, has obvious physical problems, and walks slow with great effort. Our eyes meet.

"What kind of butcher puts out crap like this?" she turns to ask me.

"Not sure what you mean," I replied.

"Look at the size of these steaks. They're skinny, have a ton of fat on them, and they're already turning gray!" she said.

"I think those are prime cuts, which always have plenty of marbling," I said.

"You think I don't know that? I was a head cook in the schools here. I am familiar with all kinds of meats," she spat at me.

"There's no sign that says you have to buy it," I offer with a smile.

"Hurumph. Well, I'm not buying any of this rubbish. My day has been bad already. I don't need to add crummy food to my troubles." She turns to stare at me straight in my face. "I could get a good deal on donuts for Saturday coffee, if someone would let me. Not everyone is aware of good places to buy stuff."

"Is that right? You'll need to come to the activity meetings and make your suggestion," I said.

"You really think anyone would listen? I doubt it. Not to mention The Terminator. She'd love to give me some back talk if I suggested getting donuts myself instead of her doing it. She'd lose a teeny bit of control and you know she wouldn't like that. Anyway, that group is just a bunch of complainers if you ask me. Speaking of complainers, I'm happy to tell you I got rid of that bitch, Jane. Haven't seen her, have ya. Well, I took care of her good. Well, I'm done here. Goodbye," she says.

Kathleen grabs her cart and goes off in another direction, but before I can answer, she turns back and yells, "Don't be in any hurry to say goodbye to me!"

I sigh. She sets you up like that. Can't be helped. She will reprimand you for something no matter how quick you are or how hard you try. Kind of like Martha, but different.

What did she mean by 'getting rid of Jane', anyhow? She didn't even acknowledge Jane is dead. What do you suppose she was really saying?

CHAPTER FOURTEEN

We finished selecting our groceries. The three of us began putting our purchases into Mary's trunk.

"Wait a minute, you guys. Janet, you put your bags to the left, Dee in the middle, and I'll put mine on the right side. Pile them in so they reach the back of the trunk so all our stuff fits, okay?" Mary instructed.

We sighed aloud as we got back into the car. "Did you guys get what you needed?" Mary asked as she turned the key in the ignition and locked the doors. Soon the air conditioner blasted out the cooled air as Mary pulled out of the parking lot.

All of us seemed satisfied with our purchases and the discounts received. I related my encounter with Kathleen.

"She was the brightest body of energy in that whole store! Get this. She said, and I quote, 'I'm happy to tell you I got rid of that bitch, Jane. Haven't seen her, have ya. Well, I took care of her good.' What do you guys think of that?" I asked.

"OMG. Another confessor. I cannot get my head around these people and their ideas," Mary said.

"We've got to pursue this and find some explanations to all of this," Janet said.

"I'll get on Manny about that camera idea," I offered. "Guess I've been a bit lax there."

"Well, once we find out what's been installed at the guard's station, you can either go to an electronics store and find out what the camera is capable of, or look it up on your computer," Mary suggested.

"I think I'll do both. First things first, though. It's going to take some doing so nobody catches us at it," I said.

"Wear black and a hooded sweater or jacket," Janet said. "No white socks, either," she added.

"Manny's the one going to do the deed, not me," I said.

"Well, then. Make sure he's dressed for the occasion," Janet said.

We were quiet after that exchange and arrived back at the gates of our paradise. Mary dropped me off first. After I removed my groceries out of her trunk, she and Janet proceeded to Mary's parking slot.

I filled the freezer with the chicken, ground turkey, and fish I purchased and put the dry goods in the cupboards after I turned on my computer. I have a low rate of MIPS per second to keep the cost bearable, and it takes several minutes before I can access the internet. Once my morning coffee reheated, I took it to my desk and sat while I waited for the internet to come up.

I was curious what kind of equipment is available for surveillance. My searches revealed there are various choices. Better to find out what make and model was mounted out there first.

It's time to give Manny a call.

Manny's wife Barbara answered the telephone. We talked for a while after she informed me that Manny wasn't home. Barbara is a great gal and I like her a lot. She assured me she would have Manny call me as soon as he returned and asked what she should tell him. I couldn't tell her, so I lied and said it was about a pool project we had in mind. Close enough. We had hatched the plan at the pool, after all.

Half-an-hour later Manny returned my call. "Now Manny, you have a habit of showing up late for things. I would appreciate it if you would show up on time."

"Late? When have I ever been late?"

"Every pancake breakfast or luncheon we have at the community center you come late."

"Oh. I guess Barbara has mentioned that to me. Well, anyway, I'll be there when you say."

I also told him what to wear. He questioned it, and I explained the need to be as indescribable and unnoticeable as possible.

After I hung up, I wondered what could go wrong.

Using my binoculars, I stood back from my patio window and focused in on the guard's station. It looked as if there was an object mounted under the roof at the front end of the building. I hadn't seen it before, although I hadn't been looking for it, either. I would explain what I'd seen to Manny tonight at the pool.

First, I had to get to the electronics store. I showed the clerk the picture I'd taken of what I thought was the camera, and he identified the equipment. He explained that today's camera's do not record, they send digital images to a computer disc or hard drive.

That means Manny doesn't have to go up and remove the camera. I texted the information to him.

***

After a light supper, I changed into my bathing suit, gathered up my towel and pool shoes and walked to the alcove by the elevator. I looked over the railing and watched the traffic whizz down the street. I enjoyed seeing the sun move over the mountains to the west when I noticed something unusual. On the white roof of the next building there was an umbrella covering one of the air conditioners. Well, I suppose they get pretty danged hot on these afternoons. I laughed to myself and took the elevator down to the first floor. I got to the pool an hour before Janet and Mary so I could talk to Manny alone.

"Did you get my text?"

"Ya. Now what are we going to do?" he asked.

Here's the deal, Manny," I started.

"You've got to use your key to get into the community room and then jimmy the lock into the office to get at the computer that records what's on the security camera," I said.

"Do you realize how hard that's gonna be?" he whined.

"You won't be in there long. Once you get in, text me, and I'll come in. I'll take care of getting a copy of what is on it."

"Then what? Sounds easy enough, if nothing goes wrong. What time are we going to do this?"

"I'm thinking three in the morning. Not much going on around here at that hour. I've been watching for a few nights."

"I'm going tell Barbara what we're doing. She could wake up if she hears me rummaging around at that hour."

"Fine. Make sure she understands why and the necessity to keep it to herself."

"Well, that's a given. She'll understand."

"Think we're all set then? Can you do it tonight? Have the clothes and such?"

"Yep. I do, in fact."

"How are we going to view what's on there?"

"I'll do it on my computer."

"Is it complicated?"

"I had a technician at the store show me how."

"Oh. How'd he know what kind it is?"

"I took a picture of it when I left to go to the electronics store. He enlarged it and was sure he knew what kind and model it is."

"Well, this should be an interesting evening, um, morning, whatever," Manny said.

I elected to go in the pool for a quick swim to cool off. Manny left without going for a dip. Mary and Janet joined me.

"You were talking to Manny for quite a while, Dee. What's the scoop?" Janet asked.

"We came up with a plan."

"And the plan is?" Mary asked.

"If I don't tell you, you won't be able to answer questions about it if someone sees us. Sorry. Better you don't know, is my opinion." I answered.

"I think you're right," Mary said. "The best I can offer is good luck."

"We might need it. I will let you know if we find out anything, though," I offered.

The three of us paddled around for a while longer until we became chilled. We got out of the pool and lounged on the chairs while the warm summer breezes brought our body temperatures back to normal.

We sat without talking for some time, tired from our workout in the water. I was the first to get up to leave.

"Be seeing you," I said as I ambled out of the gate and onto the sidewalk that led to the alcove by my elevator. As I exited, I heard my friend's well wishes and goodbyes.

I imagined what the morning hours would produce as I rode up to my floor, once again jostled by the loud bump of the gears taking me upward.

CHAPTER FIFTEEN

I changed out of my wet bathing suit, took a quick shower to rinse off the chlorine, and put on my dark brown capris with a short-sleeved dark brown top. If I had any need to join Manny out there in the dark, I wouldn't wear something light colored or bright.

I sat on a comfortable chair placed a few feet back from my patio door, with my binoculars hanging around my neck. The lateness of the hour and the swim in the pool made me sleepy. I nodded off, waking myself up when my chin hit my chest and I gave out a loud snort. I glanced over at the small old-fashioned style clock on the television console. It was two-thirty in the morning. My mouth tasted pasty as I realized how fortunate it was that I woke up before three o'clock. I looked over toward the guard's station again with my binoculars but there was nothing going on near or around the security gate area.

I went to the bathroom sink, rinsed my mouth, drank a small glass of water, and returned to my vantage point in the living room.

No sign of him yet. At 3:15 AM, I spotted Manny, moving toward the office. He did a good job getting dressed, although I didn't get a glimpse of his face.

A minute went by. Manny appeared again on the other side of the building. He must have forgotten he was to enter in through the community room.

What was he doing? I waited for my phone to show me I'd received a text message.

Oh brother. I waited another five minutes.

No reply. I sent a text with only a question mark. Again, no reply. It could only mean one thing. I must go out there to see if he made it in there or if he passed out or—? I didn't know what to think.

When I grabbed my black hooded sweatshirt and put it on, right away I felt too warm, from nerves, I guess. I went out to see for myself what happened to him.

I walked over to the office and looked around. I couldn't tell if Manny was in there.

A ping sounded on my phone. The text read: 'Come ahead."

I went to the office door. There he was, looking out at me, frowning. He put his fingers to his lips, warning me not to speak.

He opened the door and guided me toward the computer. "I think it's this one. There's two computers, but I figured they probably use one of them for the camera."

"Ya," I whispered. "Let's hope there isn't one recording us in here. You go look around while I check this out," I said.

The computer located on a separate desk had a sticker on it that read 'Security'. I sat down, loaded it with my empty disc. I had to move through recorded dates to get to the one listing the date with pictures I wanted to copy. It took too much time, so I copied all of it.

"You done yet?" Manny whispered when he came back in the room.

"Just about. Did you find any cameras in here?" I asked.

"One by the kitchen. People been stealing food out of the refrigerator in there, I hear," Manny said. "I suppose that's why it's there," he added.

"I'm done here. Let's get out," I said.

We tiptoed out of the building. Not sure why, because who would hear us? The cool night air felt good. Stealing into the office and messing with their data was risky business and I felt sweat dripping down inside my bra.

"Go on to my place, Dee. I'll meet you there in a minute. I want to check something," Manny said.

"Okay, but don't dilly dally Manny. You don't want anyone seeing you this time of the morning," I said.

I went on to Manny's apartment and when I walked onto the patio, Barbara opened the patio door and whispered to me to come in.

"Manny'll be here in a minute," I explained to her.

I sat on the couch in their living room, breathing deeply to dispel the pent-up excitement I'd felt building.

"You will never guess what happened," he whispered when Manny came in the house after several minutes.

"What in the world?" Barbara asked.

"Don't turn on any lights, Barb. Sit tight and I'll explain."

"Manny," I whispered. "What the heck happened? Have you hurt yourself?"

"Not too bad. Just a scrape."

"Are you bleeding?" Barbara asked.

"I don't know. Let me take a look," Manny answered.

Manny lifted his trouser leg to examine his leg. "It's mighty sore, and skinned up, but only a little blood."

"That's a relief," Barbara said. "How did you get hurt?"

"I was running toward my truck. Got too close to that huge boulder out there and I rammed my ankle on it," Manny said.

"Why did you want to get to your truck?" I asked.

"When we left the building, I thought I noticed movement by it. You're not going to believe this. Some young punk was trying to break into my truck. I still had the knife in my pocket I used to jimmy the door key, so I kinda pointed it at him like a gun, you know, it was in my pocket, he didn't know it wasn't a gun, and I told him to get the hell out of there. He looked scared. He ran off real fast and I watched him jump over the wall. Can you beat that? Must be in good shape to do that. I guess if you're going to break into cars on a regular basis, you'd have to be. In good shape, I mean," Manny explained.

"You're lucky he wasn't armed, Manny. There are a lot of kids these days who steal cars and have guns. You might have been a dead person," I lamented.

"I didn't want to make a lot of noise over it and then have to explain my appearance to anyone who heard a commotion and decided to investigate. I think it's great that

I was up and about to discover that hoodlum. Serendipity?" Manny suggested.

"Oh boy. We'll find out soon enough if anyone heard anything, and if they got up and looked. Well, now I have to go through all that data. I'm going home. I'm sorry you hurt yourself, Manny, and I'm thankful that kid didn't harm you. Sleep tight you guys. Get some rest before the sun comes up," I said.

I walked back home, deep in thought. I heard a patio door close, looked up and saw someone standing out there looking in my direction. My thought it was Damon, not his wife. She's much smaller than the hulk I saw. Too dark to tell for sure.

CHAPTER SIXTEEN

I slept in the next morning and fixed fried hash browns with plenty of onions, a pinch of garlic powder, a handful of frozen spinach, and over easy fried eggs. It was noon by the time I had it all prepared. I use the never stick pans that aren't supposed to have any toxic things in them so cleanup is quick and simple. I wiped my dishes and put them away.

I sat down at my computer, put in the disk and waited for the screen to come up. This wasn't going to be as easy as I'd originally thought. I was beginning to think it was encrypted. After an hour of trying to see what was recorded on the evening in question, my eyes were drying out and irritated enough to make me stop. There were other methods I could try, but not until later.

I took out my cell phone to call Mary.

"Morning, Mary. It's Dee. Thought I should report. How are you?" I asked.

"Oh, okay, I guess. I'm pretty tired. I'm about to take a nap."

"You don't sound perky, for sure. Are you okay?"

"No. It will pass," she answered. "Did anything happen last night?"

"Yes, and no. Our plan didn't work. We'll have to think of something else. You busy this afternoon?"

There was a long pause before she answered.

"Well, yes. I am awful tired. I need a nap and I have an appointment later," she said.

"You're not ill, I hope?"

"No, no. I'll be fine once I nap. Nothing interesting to tell you," she replied.

"Okay. I'll see you at the pool later, then?" I asked.

"We'll see. Bye Dee," she answered.

There's a first time for everything, I guess. Mary used to be talkative and pleasant and was neither in that conversation.

Later that afternoon, I walked over to the exercise room and rode the elliptical bike. There are windows all around the room, but are odd because you can see out from within, but when you are outside you can't see in. I was daydreaming when I noticed Damon walk by the window. He's tall and muscular, walks with an arrogant air about him, and never smiles. I got off the bike and went toward the window. He continued down the walk and made a turn to the right toward the building where Mary lives.

I wiped down the seat of the bike with an antibacterial cloth, picked up my keys and went out the exercise room door. Damon was still in my sight. If I kept far enough behind, he wouldn't know I was following. He stopped, turned, and went to the apartment in front of him. I saw the door open, and there stood Mary as she greeted Damon and let him in.

Holy Jehoshaphat! What would Mary be doing seeing Damon? I couldn't imagine.

I turned around and went home. If I'd continued walking in that direction, they may have seen me, and it would cause problems I didn't want to contemplate.

I couldn't get my mind to quit racing around the subject of Mary, and or Damon. I fixed myself a light supper, sat in my lounge chair to eat it instead of sitting at the dining table. Without thinking, I consumed what I'd prepared. My stomach didn't feel right. Upset, is what it was. I figured I might as well go to the pool and see if I couldn't get rid of the acrid feeling rising and abetting in my innards.

Janet showed up soon after I did and asked if Mary was on her way.

"I don't know. I haven't talked to her since late this morning. Not sure what she's up to," I answered.

"How did your plan work out last night, Dee?" Janet asked.

"It didn't. I have to think of something else. Let me know if you get a brilliant inspiration, though. I'm out of them at the moment," I said.

"Well, come on and get in the pool. We'll jump around and maybe something will pop into our heads," she suggested.

"Whoo! I said as I stepped in. The water is cold. Somebody turn off the heater?" I asked.

"Wow. It is cold. Maybe they forgot to pay the electric bill. Exercise faster and harder. You'll warm up quick," she said.

"Oh ya. Chilly Willy me. Guess it's worth a try," I said.

We both warmed ourselves as best we could with frantic leg and arm motions, setting the water swirling around us.

The solution was the hot tub. The light breeze chilled us further as we moved toward the tub with small quick steps.

Relief from the chills was swift.

"You look pensive," Janet remarked.

"Oh. Just deep in thought, I guess. Wondering what kind of plan we can come up with that won't end in defeat," I answered.

"I suggest you corner Mary and get her to give you all the information I think she has, not just bits and pieces," Janet said.

"Yes, that seems logical. Although I'm not sure—" I said.

The times I've been with Mary, she didn't mention Damon going to her place, she didn't reveal what her appointment was, and I believe the appointment meant Damon coming over to her apartment. She has kept the contents of that notebook to herself and given us few facts about Jane's life.

"Not sure about what?" Janet asked.

"Um. I guess I'm not sure of Mary's motives." I answered.

"Motives? Mary isn't a person who is untruthful or conniving."

"You are right. Absolutely right," I said. "I'll talk to her soon. Maybe she needs help with that notebook. There could be things in there she doesn't understand or it's too vague for her to come to conclusions. Maybe I can help by looking up stuff on the computer," I said.

"There's your plan. I don't see how you could fail with that," Janet said.

I felt warm enough in the hot tub by then, so I got out and went over to the shower to rinse off. Janet did the same when I finished. We said our goodbyes and left the area after locking the gate behind us.

I didn't sleep well once I got to bed. My frustrations with Mary gathered more and more negative thoughts until I rolled over and turned on the bedside table lamp. I swung my legs over the side of the bed and sat up until my head cleared. After a few moments of rational thinking, I concluded Mary must have reasons for seeing Damon she doesn't wish to share with me. Is it a romantic tryst? I haven't a shred of evidence to support that, other than I saw him go into her apartment. Maybe he fixes things she can't fix. Holy Hannah, I hope that's it. She may not be feeling well and not up to fixing whatever needs fixing. She hasn't been at the pool for a while and I wonder if she's upset about more than Jane's death. A talk is what we need. Gosh. She doesn't even know the camera plan didn't work.

I felt better for clearing my mind and setting a course. I turned off the light and soon fell into a deep slumber.

CHAPTER SEVENTEEN

I called Mary after I had coffee, cereal, and yogurt. The phone rang several times before she answered.

"Mary. It's Dee. How are you doing?" I asked.

I heard a yawn. "Okay, I guess. What time is it?"

"About 10 AM."

"Oh. I just woke up."

"Sorry. You doing okay?" I asked again.

"Not really. How about you?" she asked.

"I'm fine, but I'm worried about you. Did you get an appointment to see your doctor?"

"No. I haven't. Why should I do that?" she asked.

"Mary, you haven't looked well the last few times I've seen you and I'm concerned how often your face flushes," I explained.

"Oh, that. Well, it's no biggy. I feel crummy most of the time. It will pass."

"You feel okay enough for me to stop over? I have some things I want to tell you," I said.

"Gosh, Dee. I'm not up for visitors. Maybe another day."

"Tomorrow?" I pressed.

She sighed.

"Okay, then. Tomorrow. I'll see you then," Mary answered.

"I'll be there at 10. Is that okay?" I asked.

"Sure. See ya," she said as she disconnected the call.

***

I was there to ring her doorbell at 10 AM as I'd promised. When she didn't answer after two rings, I used the doorknocker.

"Who is it?" I heard her ask from the other side of the door.

"Mary, it's Dee. I said I'd be here at 10 today,"

The door opened. Mary was in her pajamas, robe, and slippers and her hair was unkempt. She walked ahead of me leading the way into the living room when she stumbled. I grabbed her arm to steady her. I heard her gasp.

"Mary, what is it? Did I hold your arm too tight?"

"No, no, Dee. I'm okay. Been working out a little with weights and I guess I'm a little sore," she explained.

I sat on her couch and watched as Mary disappeared into the kitchen.

"Coffee?" she asked when she returned.

"Thanks. That's great."

"What was it you wanted to talk about, Dee?"

"I thought I'd let you know I got Manny to agree to remove the surveillance camera from the guard house, but then I found out we didn't need to do that. Now I'm trying to figure out Plan B."

"Why would you want to remove the camera?"

"Damon told someone at coffee he saw a man coming out of the elevator in Jane's building with her on his arm the night before she died."

"Damon," she said.

I watched as her eyes looked downward and her expression looked perplexed.

"Hmm. That's interesting."

"You seem disturbed by that."

"Do I? No, I don't know what I think. Jane didn't mention anyone coming to visit, at least, not to me."

"I also wanted to know what you've read in that notebook of Jane's."

Mary looked at me as if I had asked her an out-of-bounds question. She crossed her arms tight across her chest as she spoke.

"Look, Dee. I'm not prepared to go into that right now. I'd appreciate it if you would give it a rest. I haven't read anything that is any help to finding out why she's dead and I wish you would quit asking," she said.

"Okay. Do you still want me to keep looking for ideas about what happened, or is that off limits too?"

"Just go home, Dee. Leave it be. I'm not in the mood for this," Mary said.

As I neared the door, I reached out to pat her arm to calm her down.

"Don't give me that condescending pat on the arm stuff," she barked at me.

I pulled my hand back quickly and said, "Consider me gone," as I let myself out.

I began my walk back to my apartment building. My cheeks felt hot. Her rebuke was thorough. I felt hurt. Not angry but hurt. I knew there was an explanation somewhere, and I needed to rid myself of my wounded ego first. I thought I was her friend here, her best friend. On one hand, I self-talked about getting back at her by confronting her with what I'd seen and who I saw. I'd let her have it. In my opinion, she had no business taking up with the likes of Damon. To lower herself to that degree. On the other hand, experience has told me taking high road is best. I'll resign myself to the fact she is a free woman and can make whatever decisions she wishes without my high-minded opinions. I also knew there was more to this casserole than cream of mushroom soup, and something hotter than an Arizona summer afternoon.

Back in my bedroom, I lay down for what I thought would be a few minutes. My tired mind rummaged through all the reasons to support what I believed; that she is my best friend and I am hers. Maybe Mary is a woman who needs to have sex in her life and is not content to live without it. I thought she would be more discriminating. His reputation is, oh ick. I can't imagine being desperate enough—I can't think about that. My colorful erotic dreams are enough for me.

I woke with a start and looked over at the clock on my bedside table. It was noon and I'd slept for an hour. I gazed around my room, as I do often, loving the pieces of furniture I found at various thrift stores and estate sales and some I brought with me. My favorite pieces are the desk I use as a dressing table handmade by my Dad, and the little chest of drawers which he also made from an old phonograph machine, called a Victrola. The chest of drawers was a tall piece of furniture with eight drawers, plenty to accommodate all my folded sweaters and T-shirts.

I found a long sofa table at the store to set my electronic piano on. It had several water glass stains on it when I purchased it and I removed them by rubbing it with olive oil and vinegar.

I put my shoes back on, combed my hair back in place, and headed to the kitchen to make a sandwich.

I couldn't stop thinking about Mary. What should I do or not do about her?

Before I could get the lunchmeat out of the refrigerator, a hard knock on the front door interrupted the task. Couldn't be someone I know; they'd use the doorbell.

I peeked out the tiny security glass and saw the distorted figure of Damon. Oh, damn! I opened the door about a foot.

"Damon. Hello. What do you want?"

Lord a livin' did he look ugly. He snarled at me with his yellowed teeth that had spots on them like a leopard. He was wearing shorts and a T-shirt grayed from washing it with dark clothes.

Damon pushed me out of the way and came in. I gasped, as he stood towering over me.

His hot breath stunk like something that's gone bad in the refrigerator.

"I'm here to tell you to stay out of Mary's business. You don't know what you're getting into here. I don't want to see you harassing her or telling her what to do. Do you understand?"

"I,—I don't know why you're telling me this," I said.

Damon pushed past me and went for the door. "You heard me. I'm not repeating it," he said. Out he went. He stomped. The door slammed shut.

Geez, he's a big guy. And nasty. Eyes of fire burning into me. My heart was beating fast and I don't like this one bit. First Mary's mailed threats and now Damon threatening me. What the hell?

CHAPTER EIGHTEEN

I was out for a walk the next morning. Manny came around the corner by the mailboxes the same time I did. In the sunlight, his hair glistened with the pomade he must use to keep the waves shinny. He looked like Tony Curtis in a movie from the 60's.

"Oh. Glad I ran into you," Manny said.

"That's quite a colorful outfit you have on today. Lime green shorts with walking shoes to match. So, what's up?" I asked.

He's grinning back at me like a smitten schoolboy, the flirt.

"You're looking very pretty today. Have you lost some weight?"

"Don't I wish." I changed the subject. "Manny, do you have any new information?"

"Well, I talked to Ron about the camera. Wish I'd done that first. He agreed to let me view what they have archived. I had to tell him I wanted to know who was with Jane that last night. He agreed to show me if I promised not to tell anyone. I think he's just as curious as we are. He told me the Sheriff's Department didn't find anything unusual or noteworthy.

"Wow. Well that's a step in the right direction. I won't mention it to anyone. Let me know what you find out."

I didn't tell him that I'd figured out how to view what I copied and the man with Jane that night resembled the man I saw in the grocery store parking lot. The picture wasn't as clear as I would have liked, but I got that same feeling that I did when I saw those pictures Jane had in her notebook.

"Sure, I'll keep you informed. I never talked to you about, well, you know, the stories that are going around about me. You still mad at me?"

"Should I be?"

"Well, here's the deal. Jane was having problems with Damon, and I was curious about Jane's life. I've been going over there to talk to her, Barbara knows all about this. Jane and I met at the pool several times late at night too, after you guys are out of there. There was nothing going on between us, physically. We laughed a lot; she was funny sometimes. I suppose that's when the super gossiper caught sight of us. I mean, laughing loud leads to sex, right? My Barbara gave me ideas to tell Jane how to get rid of Damon. He's a serious problem."

"Okay, Manny. I get it. But because Jane is gone, Damon will be after someone else, don't you think?" I asked.

"I suppose."

"You haven't seen him with anyone else, though, correct?"

"No. Management knows about him, according to Ron, but they have yet to issue any eviction notices to him."

"There was talk of warnings, though," I said.

"Huh. Ron didn't mention it. You heard it, though?"

"Ya. Hard to gage which is talk and which is reality."

"On another subject, you once told me you felt responsible for Jane's death. Care to explain that?"

"Well, you know how nasty she could be. One night she was caustic as all hell. I shoved her underwater in the pool and held her there. I think for too long a time. When I let her up, she had swallowed a lot of the pool water. I figure the chlorine poisoned her, you remember, they upped the amount about then, and a delayed reaction to it could have occurred the day she keeled over."

"Oh boy. Anything is possible, I guess. Do you suppose we will ever find out what the truth is?" I asked.

"Doubtful. Ron says all the files about her rental unit and any personal information are cleared out and wiped from their computers. I think that's strange."

"Manny, I'm glad you explained your situation. You sometimes say things that aren't true, but you always seemed to be a nice guy," I said.

"Thanks, I guess. What do you mean, not true? I don't make up stuff."

"Remember when you sent me an email about a certain brand of tea that researchers claimed to have urine in it? In checking the facts, I found a fake news reporting site that prints bizarre and sensational material designed to entertain, and is not in any way truthful," I said.

"Oh. I didn't know that."

"Manny. Listen. You can check out rumors you read on the internet for their veracity. Before you repeat the junk you get from friends or whatever, check it out first."

"Oh. Guess I could do that," he said.

"I'm working on another plan."

"Can you let me in on it?" he asked.

"No, not yet. It's percolating." In my head, I was telling myself not to tell Manny anything that happened with Mary, Damon, or me.

"I'm relieved to get that stuff off my chest," Manny said.

"I'm sure you are. Take care, Manny, and don't forget to check out the facts," I said.

I have a lot to think over. Another confession. Bizarre. I heard what Ron said about Jane's information being purged when I was in the office showing my kids around. Could the pool chlorine kill someone? Should I be bold and warn Mary about Damon? Then she'll know what I saw. Will she tell me what her situation is with Damon? Is the notebook a key to Jane's death? Will Mary allow me to read it?

Damon warned me to stay away from Mary, or at least not be telling her what to do. He sounded as if he would find a not so nice consequence if I did. So, how do I approach her now?

I went back home and checked my cell phone for messages. There were none. I took my keys from the hook by the front door, waved goodbye to my cat, waited for his response, his usual merp, and left the building after locking my door.

My little blue car was hot inside, even though the temperature outside was nice at 87 degrees. My parking space gets full sun most of the day even though there is a metal canopy above it. I noticed a piece of paper stuck in the windshield wiper. I turned on the air conditioner, opened the door, and retrieved the sheet of paper.

Big bold letters in red got my attention. "Consider This A Warning!"

What the heck? Mary received notes containing the same phrase. What am I being warned about? I can't say I'm feeling any too good about being selected along with Mary. She got a note in the mail, but someone close enough to where we live put a note on my car. Someone knows where I live and where I park. I am major upset. I sat in my car with the air conditioner running for several minutes. I needed to think. I'm a target along with Mary and the reason why is not clear. Neither of us have done anything to warrant such drastic measures. Did the both of us rebuff someone's advances? Did we make remarks at coffee that made someone angry and wanting to exact some kind of vengeance? What else could there be?

I can't change what just happened, but I can change the scenery and stop, for the moment worrying about things I can't control. I backed out of my space and headed for the thrift stores on the corner of Thrift Lane and You Can't Live Without It Drive. I needed to think about other things. Such as, what I need to fill the blank spots on my walls. I may even consider curtains or drapes to bring color into the endless expanse of whiteness of the walls. Oh man, let these kinds of thoughts blot out the fright I'm feeling.

The thrift stores entrances were wide open and welcoming signs begged for my attention. The array of garments hanging in wait for a new possessor of the latest in castoffs becomes overwhelming because of its sheer volume. I cannot decide with so many choices before me. I move on to another store. There is furniture of all sizes and quality housed within the small businesses lining the streets. Nothing interested me there. The miniscule odor of neglect and age erupts in greater proportion as I wander further into the depths of the repositories of dining and bedroom sets found in the back rooms of cavernous warehouses located down the street from the clothing stores. There are dining table pads stacked to the ceiling on a marred and unusable table. Lamps adorn living room tables exhibiting every size, color, and era of presumed beauty. One small piece catches my eye, a piano stool. The old-fashioned kind. It swivels and is made of oak. I can remember wanting one for years. But now, age advancing, and my girth, I am aware of impending discomfort if I buy it. Like it or not, my age requires the padded seat. I move on to admire a beautiful, tall chest of drawers. The owner approaches me.

"You like this piece?" he inquires. His voice is low and sounds sweet with a hint of an accent. "There is a headboard and matching bedside tables."

"I have a small home. I think the tall chests of drawers are a good way to go. Up, not out. Uses less wall space."

"Yes, but you must consider this. You are not tall enough to see what is in the top drawer. This piece is taller than most. Try it. You will see," he tells me.

I could reach the drawer pulls and I could pull it open without effort, but I couldn't see the contents and would not have a clue, much less remember, what was in the top drawer.

"I see. You are right."

"We have plenty of other sets with not so tall chests. Do you want to see?" he asks.

"I guess not. Not today, but thank you."

I left the shop, knowing I hadn't looked for pictures for my walls. The time spent, however, had given me the gift of relief from the stress of unanswered questions and the fear of being watched and targeted for consequences for an unknown misdeed.

When I returned home, I called Janet and she asked if I would come over to her place.

"You look wonderful, Janet. What a great outfit. Love the green on you. Sorta sagey in color, huh?"

"Thanks. Dee, I'm so glad you came over. I need to talk to you about my family."

"What's going on, Janet?"

"You know my brother, Tony, well, he's had bad news about his wife, and he shared it with me today."

"Oh dear. I'm sorry, Janet. He's the one who lives in Chandler?"

"Yes. His wife has Alzheimer's disease. He learned of it two years ago and never told me. Anyway, she's showing disturbing tendencies."

"Did you notice any problems when you visited?"

"Sort of. She seemed forgetful. Repeated things. I didn't put it together until Tony called me today."

"I know you don't get together often, but maybe you could have supported him if he had informed you earlier."

"Yes, but I think pride gets in the way. I believe he sees me as the older, smarter sister and needs to compete."

"That aside, do you think he'll accept help from you now?"

"I doubt it. I offered; he refused. It's what he said later in our conversation that has me worried."

"What did he say?"

"She has a gun. He gave it to her years ago for her protection when he traveled because of his job. She still has it, loaded, by her bedside. That alone isn't so alarming. What worries me is that fact that Tony described her increasing bad temper. She goes off on a tangent that relates to nothing."

"Combine that with a loaded gun. Did you suggest he get rid of the gun?"

"Yes, I did. I'm driving down there tomorrow to pick it up. I'm sure I can find a buyer. It is a valuable piece."

"Good. That's good. I'm glad he agreed to let you take it. It will be a relief once it is out of their house."

"Yes. I already have a buyer."

"I'm so sorry this has happened. Your brother is a great guy. He has a life filled with difficult decisions ahead of him."

"I hope he will at least call more often and talk with me. His wife controls the roost, always has. He has always gone along with whatever she decides, because I think he's nuts about her. I wonder if he'll be able to stand up to her when and if she gets unruly."

"Did you suggest he keep in touch more often?"

"Yes. I think he will."

"You may have to start the calls. Janet, this situation reminds me of a seminar I attended at the place where my Mother was living. I still have pamphlets I can give you. I remember the speaker talked about the moral responsibility of the caregiver to keep themselves and the loved one safe. What caught my attention was his suggestion that a caregiver could be held accountable morally if the patient caused his own death or someone else's. I don't mean to say, legally responsible, you understand."

"No, I get it. You're right. Wow. That's a scary thought. Thanks for mentioning it. Yes, I'll appreciate the information, and I'll talk with Tony about it. On another subject, have you seen or talked to Mary the past few days? I haven't seen her for weeks."

"No, I haven't. I'm worried about her. It is time for me to reconnect. Maybe I shouldn't have waited this long."

"Let's plan a get-together. We haven't been out to dinner in a long while."

"Good idea. I'll call her, or go over there, and let you know. How about a movie and then dinner?"

"Sure. That sounds good. Thanks for listening. I'm worried."

"I know you are, Janet. Anytime you want to talk, you know where I am," I said as I left. I didn't think the time was appropriate to tell her about the warning I'd received.

"Say, why don't we go to the pool after supper tonight? I'll call and see if Mary will meet us there," Janet suggested.

"OK. Six-thirty tonight good with you?"

"Yep." I couldn't tell her what kind of day I'd had. She had enough of a problem on her mind.

Janet smiled at me as I left and I felt my stomach rumble as I headed back to my place. She must have been cooking before I got there. The aromas had disturbed my hunger parts.

CHAPTER NINETEEN

I found a bowl of mac and cheese in the freezer and heated it in the microwave. My breakfast dishes sat in the sink and since there were few, I saved them up to wash them with my dinner utensils. Hand washing dishes provides a much needed time for me to think. Having my hands in warm water is beneficial too. It helps to relieve the stiffness that occurs from time to time. Tonight I rummaged through my feelings, enacting scenes in my head about how I would talk to Mary the next time I saw her. I feel guilty I've not spoken to her in about two weeks. Tomorrow. Or maybe she'll show up at the pool. I hope sleep and tomorrow will bring wisdom to my dulled and tired brain.

Janet was at the pool when I got there, but Mary didn't show.

"Did you get in touch with her?" I asked.

"No answer. We'll keep trying."

We spent about a half-hour swimming and exercising and then headed for our towels on the chaise lounges.

"I was just thinking of the time you and I went to the speed dating event. Remember?" Janet said.

"Ya. That was pretty interesting. Mary didn't want to do it. Did she ever say why?"

"Nope. I think she's shy," Janet offered.

I wondered, after witnessing Damon's visit to Mary's.

"Remember what it was like when we were sitting by the entrance waiting for our assigned meeting tables?" I said.

"Oh my gosh. The men came in, one by one. We were in the wrong neighborhood for sure. They were a tired, sorry looking bunch. Divorce and widowhood did them no favors,"

"However, once we talked to them, a few stood out, don't you think?"

"Yes. I remember, while we sat and waited I asked if you wanted to make a run for it! We decided to stay and both of us talked to a couple of fellows that were nice. It shows you can't judge a parcel by the stamp."

"For sure."

We sat silent for a moment.

"Uh, Janet, I just thought of something. The one man who actually dressed for the occasion, think back. Anything come to mind?"

"Hmm." Janet turned toward me with an enlightened expression on her face. "Oh for Pete's sake. He was the second driver when we ha, ha, toured Daystar City!"

"My thought exactly. How'd we miss that?"

"I don't think I really looked at him closely. The car, hat, and the cigar, those things stood out."

"He didn't say much either. Grunted, as I recall."

"He didn't say anything to me. I had to make all the conversation," I commented.

"There's a puzzle here and we are missing a lot of pieces, Dee. I don't think I have the ability to sort any of it out. Too much else on my mind with my brother's troubles and, you know what? I had a hissy fit all by myself today because I've just had it with looking at my crooked screen door on the patio."

"Did you put in a request to have it fixed?"

"Guess I could do that instead of fussing."

"Well, I've got to get to bed, Janet. I am beginning to feel even more tired than when I got here. We'll work out the puzzle somehow. Call maintenance and stay in touch," I said as she went out the pool gate.

***

Morning burned bright and hot, unprecedented warmth for a late October day. I showered, fixed my hair, and found my face in the pretty box filled with cosmetics on my vanity. My radio burgeoned with a violin player plucking notes across the strings of the instrument sounding like running water or a small waterfall trickling on its way down on the rocks to a pool below. Lovely. Soothing. Happy sounds. I could dress and feel ready for the day.

When I called Mary, I was prepared to be pleasant and accepting of whatever she told me. I didn't get the chance. She did not answer my phone call and she did not respond to my voicemail.

I went to Mary's and knocked on her door. No answer. I walked around to her patio intending to look in the glass doors. The blinds were closed. I went back to the front door and knocked harder. Still no answer. I pulled out my keychain and selected the key she'd given me for emergency situations figuring this was such an occurrence. I pushed open the door and called her name, not loud enough to alert her neighbors. As I turned and closed the door behind me, I locked it from the inside. I called out in a soft voice at first, but the dead quiet left me unsettled. Her bedroom door was ajar and I pushed it open and peeked in.

She hadn't made her bed and it was a mess, uncharacteristic for Mary. I walked further into the room, scanning all the corners, calling her name, praying I wouldn't find a body somewhere on the floor. I opened the closets. Nothing. The floors were clear of bodies. When I reached the other side of the bed, I reeled at the sight of what I saw near her pillow. Blood. It wasn't a bright red, and it didn't look wet. Must have been there a while.

I sucked in air because I didn't want to faint. When I returned to the living room, I took my cell phone out of its holder and dialed 911.

"No body. Just blood. She's not here. Hurry."

While waiting for the Sheriff, I examined the rest of the place. There isn't a lot of space; she only has one bedroom. I hadn't looked in the bathroom. I was thankful to find the shower curtain open. Nothing out of place and no body in the tub. Mary's cat, Pepper was not there to greet me. That felt strange. He was usually at the door to greet you.

In the living room, I sat and waited, shivering from frightful thoughts. I shoved myself back into the couch cushions, hoping for comfort. Something felt hard between the cushion and the arm. I pulled out a notebook. Oh gad! It's THE notebook. I shoved it in my jeans under my belt and pulled my shirt out to cover it up. It was uncomfortable. I heard the sirens and went to unlock the front door.

The officers came, were thorough, and asked questions. I explained to them how Mary and I had become close friends. I divulged knowing about threats she'd received, knowing they would come across that information themselves as Mary had reported it. I knew of no living relatives to contact. After a long search of the premises, they told me her car was parked in its place. They'd found small drops of blood leading to the parking area nearest the blacktop leading out of the complex. A woman with gauze shoe covers took samples and she removed the bottom sheet and mattress pad from Mary's bed.

They found Mary's cat Pepper hiding in the front door closet. I told them Mary's next-door neighbor often took care of him and they could take him there. Pepper jumped into the officer's comforting arms and offered a lick and a nuzzle. He would be fine.

I begged for permission to leave. They figured I had nothing more to report and agreed I could go but to remain in the area in case they needed to talk again.

I left Mary's, shaken and afraid for what might come next. It seemed as if all the neighbors in the complex were standing about with questioning looks on their faces as I walked by. I shook my head 'no' and said a hundred and fifty-two times, 'Mary's not there. I don't know what happened.'

Great relief came when I closed my door and shut out any possible intrusion.

I sat on my lounge chair, pulled the notebook out from my jeans, and my cell phone. There were two messages, one from Janet and one from Manny. I returned Janet's call, told her what happened and she asked to come over. I put the notebook in my bedroom, thinking it was something I wanted to take a long look at in private before sharing its contents. Maybe it's nothing.

I called Manny to explain what I had seen and done and gave him a stern warning not to tell anyone what I'd told him. He promised to keep our conversation confidential but explained that he would have to confide in Barbara. I knew the information would remain safe with her. I asked him to keep snooping around at odd hours by Mary's to see if there was any kind of activity we should know about.

"Won't there be officers around there wondering what I'm doing?" he asked.

"If there is, just tell them you're out for a walk, stiff legs and such. You know," I answered.

"This is scary. First, Jane, now Mary. I don't know what to make of this," he lamented.

"Well, we know Mary is missing. We don't know Jane's fate because we have no evidence that she is dead. It is peculiar for two people from the same complex to have experienced serious events like this. I think somebody took Mary, conked her on the head, and carried her out. I am hoping somebody saw it happen or saw someone and can give a description. The frustration is that I can do nothing to help either one of them." I said.

"Keep in touch, Dee, and you keep your eyes peeled too."

As soon as I hung up my doorbell chimed and I let Janet in.

CHAPTER TWENTY

Janet and I talked for a long while, conjuring up possibilities.

"She's injured, that's for sure. The head bleeds a lot and maybe she's okay and just has a headache," Janet offered.

"Yes, but someone *took* her. She wouldn't have waltzed out of there on her own power with an injury like that," I said.

"Maybe she fell and bumped her head hard enough to bleed, decided to rest and then when she woke up she figured she needed attention for her wound."

"Her phone was there. I checked it. No calls were placed to anyone before I went in."

"How'd you get into her phone?"

"No security code. You know Mary, she uses it for Dr. appointments and to call us. She doesn't know how to add a code to her phone, I'm sure."

"I'm surprised. Oh my. What a limited life. Such a sweet, great person. We'll help her with it when she gets back."

"I like how you're thinking positive."

"Someone had to take her for some help with that wound. I bet if we checked the emergency places and the Urgent Care Centers we'd find out where she is," Janet suggested.

"You think? Hmm. Go on my computer and get the numbers. I'll make the calls."

"Don't you think the Sheriff's Department has already done that?" Janet asked.

"Oh. Ya. I suppose. Back to square one. I don't know what to do. How about some coffee, or will it keep you up tonight?" I asked.

"That sounds so good. And I don't care if I am."

I made coffee and I brewed it stronger than usual. The pungent odor filled my living room. We sipped and thought, coming up with more theories as time passed.

"Maybe she wandered off forgetting who she is and where she lives," I said.

"There again, I would guess the authorities have put out a description and a look out for her."

"Yes. They asked for a picture. I had one on my phone. I emailed it to the department's email."

"Oh, good. What about that notebook, Dee? You should use your key and go in there and find it."

"I found it, Janet. I have it here."

"For real?"

"Yes."

"Let's read it then. It could help."

I sighed. "I'd rather read it myself and then go over it with you. Do you mind?"

"I guess not. Now, don't keep stuff to yourself like Mary did. Look where it got her?"

"You think it's connected?"

"Can't rule it out."

"I suppose."

"Hey. I talked to Tony this morning."

"How's things going with your brother?"

"Not good. Lorraine, his wife, realized her gun was gone and threw a holy maloney fit. He's asked me to get the gun back from the buyer."

"No."

"Yes."

"You going to do it?"

"I think I have to."

"Oh, Janet. No. You—you need to think this through."

"I know."

My fingers went to my lips to seal off any attempt to moralize. "I'm so sorry it has come to this."

"I know," she repeated. "I've stayed too late I think. We haven't been able to figure out how to help or find Mary, and I sure as hell don't know how to help my brother to understand how he is putting himself and his wife in danger."

"Wait, just a second." I returned with the pamphlets from the Alzheimer's seminar I'd attended and pressed them into Janet's hands. "These are the pamphlets I told you about. Maybe they will inspire you."

"Thanks, Dee. You're a good friend."

I closed the door taking in Janet's somber expression with hopefulness in my heart for both Janet and her brother.

I sat in my chair again, scratched my head, and let thoughts ramble. I called Manny on my cell phone.

"Manny, it's Dee. Bring Barbara with you and let's get in your truck and start searching. You in?"

"At this hour?"

"Manny. It's only eight o'clock."

"Ya, I know. But it's an hour before my bedtime."

"Hey. How often did you go to the pool after nine o'clock in the evening?" I asked.

"Oh. Ya. Well."

"It's important Manny. We've got to at least try to find Mary."

"Oh. That's what you have in mind. That's different. Gimme fifteen minutes. I'll pick you up in front of your building."

"Thanks, Manny. Make sure your cell phone's charged."

"Got it."

I grabbed my hooded zip-up sweatshirt, my phone, and my keys and headed out to the blacktop where Manny would be waiting. October nights can become chilly for this Arizona, thinned out blood person who feels the coolness sooner than most.

Manny's wife greeted me and slid closer to Manny to make room for me in the front seat. It's a big truck, wide and purchased new. Manny takes great pride in his vehicle and the night someone tried to steal something out of the back of his truck gave him several nights of apprehension.

"Where're we off to, Dee?"

"Northern Daystar City. Remember, you said you thought you knew where that ding-dong had taken us?"

"Oh ya. What do you suppose we are looking for?"

"Haven't a clue, Manny, but for some reason, I'm thinking there's a connection to all these unusual things that have been happening."

"What things?" Barbara asked.

"Well, I've felt someone watching me, and that person looked so much like a photo I saw of Jane's son. Both Mary and I have received creepy notes printed in bright red giving us a warning. I don't think I told you, Manny, but Damon threatened me, ordering me to stay out of Mary's business."

"No. You didn't tell me. I didn't know about the warnings either."

"There is something ominous going on. Jane's disappearance, her place cleaned out the same day, and now Mary is hurt and missing. I think it adds up to something bad."

"I didn't know about Jane's apartment being cleaned out," Barbara commented. "How'd you know about that?"

"Well, this goes no further. Mary had a key that Jane gave her and we went in there looking for things Jane wanted Mary to have. It was bare to the bones."

"Huh. That's weird. Did you find what you were looking for?" Barbara asked.

"Sort of. Well, I guess we did. There were pictures and a notebook. I haven't read the notebook yet."

"I would have thought you would have read that notebook before we started traipsing around tonight," Manny said.

"Ya, but I'm so worried about Mary that I felt I had to do something more concrete to find her."

"We'll see whatever it is we are going to see," Manny stated. "Here we are, Dee. Any of this area seem familiar?"

"Yes, yes it does. See the trees up that way? That's the park we walked to."

Manny drove at a slow speed while we went past the homes in the area.

"Will you look at that!" Manny said. "That's Damon's truck, right there, parked in front of that stucco house."

My eyes were wide open at that point. "Sure looks like his truck. What the heck would he be doing here?" I asked.

"I'm gonna pull over into the park's lot here. You guys sit tight. I'll meander by that house to see if I can see anything."

"You better hope Damon doesn't come outside and see you," I said.

"Maybe I won't get real close," Manny answered.

Barbara and I sat in silence for a few minutes. Then I told her about our unscheduled side trip to this area when the three of us had gone on the history tour of Daystar City.

"Manny told me a little about that. You must have been scared," Barbara said.

"Yes and no. Guess we were too busy making sure we got to safety and stayed out of eyesight of the creep who drove us there."

Manny came back to the truck and got in.

"There's quite an argument going on in that house. Damon is in there. Can't mistake that voice of his. I'm telling you, those people are yelling at each other. Only words I could make out were 'she is not'. Who knows what that means, "Manny explained.

"We can't just let it go at that, Manny. Let's you and me go back there, and see if we can peep in there. Barbara, you stay here. Cough real loud if you see anyone come out any doors, okay?" I said.

"I don't know if this is such a good idea—" Barbara said.

We were already out of the truck and up the sidewalk nearing the front of the house. I hand signaled Manny to go around the front while I went to the side.

I could see into the home between the slats of the blinds. Looked like the dining room. There were at least four people in the room. The two voices I heard belonged to men. I moved closer to the house to get a look at the women. They were sitting together on a couch. My jaw dropped in shock. Both women had material covering their faces. Then the men were yelling and one was coming toward the window. I crouched and closed my eyes. I suppose I thought if I couldn't see them, they couldn't see me. My breaths came in short gasps. I wondered where Manny was and if he saw anything. Then I heard him psssting at me. I opened my eyes and put my finger to my lips. He signaled me to follow him. I couldn't see his face, but I assumed he didn't know there was someone by the window and I couldn't get up at that moment. So, I crouched down and stayed in place.

Next thing I knew there was a lot of commotion inside the house. "Manny, get over here," I whispered.

Manny crept up next to me. "Now what?" he asked.

"Shh. Something's going on. Press up against the house and stay still," I said, crouching down into myself.

Seconds later, the garage door opened up and a black SUV sped out from its interior with no lights guiding it down the short driveway.

"Lord a livin'," I whispered. I hope Barbara has her head down. Then I heard her cough.

"She's paying attention. That's good. I don't hear the car anymore. Why don't you go back there and tell her everything's okay. I'm going to nose around here since everyone seems to be gone," I said.

"Don't be long. It may not be safe," Manny said.

I stood up and stretched. I was wobbly. Been a long while since I remained in a position like that for any length of time. I stood on my tiptoes and looked back in the room. Everything looked dark. I took a long look at the window. It was a crank-out type and was slightly ajar and low enough I could almost get a knee up on the sill. I pushed hard on the frame of it and tried to push myself up. I didn't succeed. I got back in place, wishing I was in better shape. I attempted to get up on the sill again. Only some of me was on it because it wasn't all that big. I was sure it was an old window because it pulled open without a lot of effort. I yanked, and the opening became nice and wide. I pushed the screen to the inside, and waited to see if the noise of it hitting the floor would be noticed. I couldn't be positive the house was empty. I grabbed onto the sill and the frame and pulled myself in as far as I could. I started to sweat with the exertion, but one more lurch forward and I was on my belly on the sill. I had to stop a second and get my breath. I pulled one leg up and managed to fall down into the room. It didn't feel very good when I hit the floor on top of the screen. Not good to fall onto. I laid there, wondering if I could get up from the floor. I've had trouble doing that in the past. The screen was mighty uncomfortable. This wasn't the best time to be lying there. I hurt. I got myself up, but I was slow in doing so. It was hard to see without light. I pushed the curtain back and the streetlights helped illuminate the room. I walked toward the back of the house and found myself in the kitchen. Then I wondered what I thought I would do in there, and headed back into the living room. Just as my foot turned, I heard muffled voices. It sounded as if they were coming from a room near the rear of the house. Oh boy. I knew I had to get out of there pronto.

Wherever the conversation was taking place, it was getting louder and I heard footsteps coming closer. If I was to be found out, that was a heck of a motivator. I scurried back to the window.

It was more difficult to get back out of it than getting in. As I struggled, I realized a better solution and hauled myself back in. I went to the front door or at least to the wall where I thought it was, and I felt my way along until I came to it. One of the tables at the front of the room helped to keep me upright. There was something, a piece of paper, I thought, on the table, under my hand. I put it in my pocket and kept going. Finally, I found a doorknob. I hoped it wasn't a door to a bedroom. I turned the handle and the night air greeted my burning face and body. I didn't bother closing it, because the voices were getting louder.

I moved as fast as I could toward the truck, slipped on the gravel in the yard, regained my balance and kept going. It was hard to move fast with fear rising in my chest, the injury I'd already received when I fell in the room, and my compromised old woman strength as I realized I could be caught by the persons chasing after me. Good old adrenalin came to my rescue and I was able to get to the truck. I heard someone yelling at my backside.

"Hey, what in the hell do you think you're doing," I heard a man's voice shouting.

I looked back to see he was standing in the doorway, not chasing after me as I'd thought.

"Get back here, you—" he didn't finish the sentence or I couldn't hear it.

I opened the truck door, slid in, and said, "go" as loud as I could muster, happy Manny got back in the truck before I did. I barely had the door closed as Manny floored the gas pedal and off we went. I straightened myself up and fiddled around until I got the seat belt secured around me.

"Geez, Dee. What in the heck took you so long?" he asked.

"Uh, well, I crawled in through the side window," I answered, breathing hard.

"You what? Oh my god. You are one nuts person," Manny said.

I moaned a little, the ache in my back and knees giving me major discomfort.

"You hurt yourself. Where?" Barbara asked.

"My back and my knees. I fell on the screen on the floor when I shoved my way in. Shouldn't have done that," I said.

"I'll say. You going to be okay? And what, by the way, did you find, if anything in that house?" Manny asked.

"Nothing. I wanted so bad to find something that would help us find Mary, but there were people still in

195

there. I heard voices and that's when I got the heck out of there."

"You are damned lucky they didn't find you. This night could have ended badly for you," Manny said.

"Ya, ya. I know. One of them was yelling at me as I ran."

"You got your breath back?" Manny asked.

"Ya."

"Tell me what you saw when you were still outside of the house."

"There were two men in there and two women. Both sitting on the couch and they each had a thing or something over their mouths, like a blindfold. The light was too dim to figure out if either one of them was Mary. The blindfolds were large. Covered most of their heads. The men were yelling at each other. Couldn't make out their conversations. My hearing must not be so good."

"We're going to have to call the Sheriff's Department and tell them about this. Even if it is nobody we know, someone in there is in trouble. And we know Damon is involved."

"Well, you recognized his voice, but I didn't hear enough to confirm that. However, it is his truck out there.

"Did you write down his license number and the house number?" I asked.

"Barbara did. I'm going to drive by there again to see if there's any change or lights back on, or, oh, I dunno," Manny said. He turned back and drove toward the house.

"Damon's truck is gone. The lights in the house are out. Either they are still in another room of the house, or they've all left," Barbara said.

"There's still people in there, believe me. Now what do we tell the Sheriff?" I asked.

"What we saw and what happened," Manny answered.

"You're not going to tell them I went in there," I cautioned.

"No. Wouldn't that be breaking and entering?"

"I 'spose."

I massaged my knees and arms as we drove back to Winter Gardens saying nothing more.

CHAPTER TWENTY-ONE

"Come on over to our place, Dee. We'll call the Sheriff together," Manny proposed.

"Okay. Boy. What time is it? I'm exhausted," I said.

"Me too," Barbara said. "I'll fix us some hot cocoa. Maybe that will perk us up."

"That would be great," I said.

Manny parked and we slid out of the truck seat and walked to their building. I limped. Barbara went to the kitchen and Manny sat down opposite me in the living room with his phone in his hand. "Well, here we go," he said as he tapped the numbers into his cell phone.

I have to say Manny did a right fine job of explaining what we had just done, saying it was just a hunch I'd had and we hadn't expected anything to come of it. His conversation with the Sheriff sounded like he didn't have to defend our actions. Manny made clear the suspicious circumstances and the need for their attention.

"They got Damon's license number and I bet they'll be talking to him soon," Manny said after he disconnected the call.

"Did they sound angry?"

"No. Matter-of-fact. They seemed, like, well, alarmed when I told them about the blindfolds on the women. Wanted to know more. But, you were the one who saw them, not me. I'm sure they sent personnel out to that address already. I sure hope they'll tell us what they find," Manny said.

"Oh, that's doubtful. They hold investigations and information pretty tight, don't you think?" I said.

Barbara came in from the kitchen with a tray filled with three cups of steaming hot chocolate with miniature marshmallows floating on top.

"Boy does that smell delicious," I said.

"Here you go. Have at it," Barbara said when she put the tray on the coffee table.

I got up and went to get a cup for myself, and then handed one to Manny and Barbara.

The room was quiet. I couldn't leave it that way for long.

"How's your leg, Manny. I forgot to ask you about it when you scraped it on the boulder.

"I had to get a tetanus shot the next day. I went to Urgent Care because the scrape was deeper than I first thought."

"Did I ever tell you about the time I had to take my cousin's son to the doctor for a tetanus shot?" I asked.

"Umm, no, I don't think you did. But I'm sure you will now," Manny said.

"Well, this kid is what you'd call squeamish, over sensitive, is a sweet boy, but could be a pain in the backside. He was running barefoot and caught a small tree branch between his big toe and the next one. It put a small gash in there. So, I rinsed it while he screamed, put a towel around it and headed for the Doctor's office. Thankfully, they took us right in. So the kid is sitting in a chair on one side of the room, the doctor comes in with the syringe in hand for a tetanus shot, starts to go toward the kid, and the boy starts screaming. The doctor looks at him and says, 'look son, I'm over here, nowhere near you, where I can't possibly hurt you.' There was a long pause, the kid quits screaming and looks straight up at the doc and says, 'ya, but you'll be close to me any second now' and starts yelling again. Can you beat that?" I said.

Manny, Barbara and I laughed and then we stared down at our empty cocoa cups.

"I should leave. It's late and I'm feeling mighty tired. Thanks for the cocoa and thanks for driving there, Manny. I can't imagine where this is all going,"

"Goodnight, Dee. We'll be in touch," they both said.

I am tired, and my knees still hurt, but I knew I wouldn't be able to fall asleep right away. After I put on my pajamas and shoved my feet into the soft, warm material in my slippers, I poured a glass of water, swallowed my evening pills, and sat in my lounge chair and turned the back massager on. Remembering I had put the notebook in my bedroom, I got up and retrieved it.

I opened it and read. I yawned after a long while and paused. The information was interesting, but so far it shed no light on recent events. Next thing, my chin bounced off my chest and I gave out my usual snort. I put the notebook down and crawled into bed. My cat was already there and greeted me with a sleepy merp.

***

The next morning I picked up where I left off reading the notebook. There were numerous notes concerning Jane's family. I found newspaper clippings tucked in between some of the pages. They referred to reports of women paraded in the streets of France as traitors at the end of World War II because they had consorted with

German soldiers. I looked at the picture with the article. The woman bore a strong resemblance to Jane. I figured it wasn't Jane's mother. Maybe it's her grandmother.

Further into the notebook I saw another newspaper article that chronicled the life and death of a prominent business owner in Chicago who was about to testify against members of the mob. He was found dead a week before making his courtroom appearance. I figured that must have been Jane's mob husband.

Reading these notations didn't bring me any closer to understanding why Jane disappeared along with her belongings and how it connected to Mary. I suppose if the mob learned where she was, they could be the ones after her. But the men in suits didn't add up to mob. They didn't look the part. Besides, I don't see Damon as a mobster. He's big, dumb and uncouth, but not smart enough to keep his pants on. That implies that mobsters do, and I don't know that for fact. Jane and Mary were friends, but nothing in the notebook points to the need to eliminate them from this earth.

I washed up, got dressed, and made myself presentable. I called Manny. Barbara answered.

"I'm going back in Mary's, Barbara. I thought it best that I tell someone. Let Manny know, Okay? I'm hoping no one will notice me going in there."

"Well, it's lunch time. People are home and it is their nap time, so you should be okay," Barbara commented.

"Would you tell Manny I'd like him to join me there? I'd feel better with someone else with me. I don't think I'll be long. Figure I'll need, maybe an hour," I told her.

"Sure, I'll tell him. He should be here any minute now," she said.

No one was outside or in the area as I put her key in the door. I closed it without making noise. The air smelled stale. She gets sun in the morning, but with all the drapes drawn, it still felt warmer than usual.

I went right to her bedroom. I saw a small stain left on the mattress where the sheet and mattress pad had been removed. It gave me a dull pain in my gut. The small bedside table had two drawers and I opened them and took out their contents. In there I found a stack of papers in each drawer. I took them all with me to the living room and sat on her couch.

I felt funny pawing through her personal things. She had insurance documents, one year's tax returns, all the papers we have to keep on hand all neat and separated into folders marked with their contents.

I didn't find more notes or articles of further interest, until I came to a manila envelope with a clasp. I bent it open, pulled out two documents, and read the information on them. Both had a notary public stamp.

I put them back into the envelope and bent the clasp shut. My mind raced with thoughts as I tried to put the information I'd just seen into some kind of logical conclusion.

A sound coming from outside startled me and I got up from the couch and went to the china hutch. I lifted the silverware chest and shoved all the papers under it. As I moved toward the front window, I heard someone fiddling with the door handle. Probably Manny. I started toward the door to open it for him.

The front door flew open and Damon came flying through. Damn. Manny should've been here. He came at me with rhythmic steps pounding on the carpet. It wasn't like 'The March Of The Teddy Bears' but more like the latter notes you'd hear in 'The Sorcerer's Apprentice'.

Hard heavy steps and I anticipated nothing good about to happen right now.

He pushed the door shut and was on me before I could blink. He spoke in a monotone. "I told you to keep out of Mary's business. Now I'm going to teach you a lesson." His fist hit my jaw and that's all I remember.

CHAPTER TWENTY-TWO

I woke up in a hospital bed, confused. Manny and Barbara stood at the side of the bed.

"Welcome back to our world," Barbara said.

Piercing pain in my head and face forced an ugly expression on my face.

"Don't talk. They think your jaw is broken. They'll be up to take you for X-Rays any minute now."

"Uhh," about all I could accomplish.

"How'd this happen? Do you know?" Manny asked.

I whispered Damon's name.

"Damon! Damn. I'm calling the Sheriff to let them know. I'll be right back," Manny said as he dashed out of the room.

Barbara stepped closer and took my hand. "I'm so sorry Manny was too late to be there in time to stop what happened. He's never on time for anything,"

I nodded a 'yes'.

"Manny went over to Mary's as soon as he got home, saw the door open, walked in, and found you. He called the ambulance. Good thing your purse was there and it had all the information they needed so they could call your doctor and all that," Barbara said.

"Huh," was all I could manage. I made a bunch of motions like poking my arm with a syringe suggesting I'd like a shot to help with the pain.

"I'll get a nurse. Hang on," she responded.

It seemed a long time before I got relief. My doctor informed me the break wasn't complicated and they will perform a procedure to keep my jaw in place.

They put bands on my molars to restrict movement and allow the simple break to heal. I left the hospital the next day with instructions to have a wire cutter and scissors handy in case I choke or have to vomit. The paper list also said I have to support my chin if I need to sneeze or yawn. Food will be a challenge. Lots of shakes are listed on the sheet, and pureeing vegetables sounds awful. How can it taste good when it will look unappetizing?

Manny and Barbara were at the hospital's entrance awaiting my discharge. The nurse brought me down in a wheelchair. They informed me that Janet was waiting for me at my place.

"Oh brother! It's my fault you look like this," Manny said.

"Boy! You do look a sight. Have you seen yourself in the mirror?" Barbara asked.

"Uh, no, why would I want to do that?" I said with a voice that is terse, even though I'm not angry. You can speak and people can understand you as long as you use your tongue to help pronounce your words.

Janet held up a mirror in front of me.

"Egad. Those are spectacular bruises, huh," I managed. "Well, what delightful combination did you come up with for my lunch that goes through a straw?"

"Soup, chicken soup," she answered.

"I guess you didn't know that's all I've had since, oh, whenever I got fed the first time."

"Sorry. I should have asked. The broth is homemade and I'm sure it'll be better than what you had."

"You think?" I sighed. The drugs haven't worn off and I'm tired and hungry.

Relief swept over me during the ride home realizing I had a fair chance of sipping a broth that would taste a lot better than the hospital's rendition.

Wobbly legs propelled me over the sidewalk and to the elevator with Manny giving support on one side and Barbara on the other. They guided me expertly in the door and into a chair at the dining table.

I sat and she tied a bib on me. "Huh?" I asked.

"Soup can spill even if it's going through a straw. Just be careful. Now, if it's too hot, wait for it to cool. I don't want you coughing or something terrible like that."

"Ya." I tried it and it was satisfactory. I didn't feel like telling her it was much better than the hospital's soup. I was crabby and I wasn't going to apologize for it. I learned to go slow, swallow a little at a time. It seemed to take forever to eat.

About a half hour later, I finished. Janet had some too, but she finished first.

"Now what would you like?"

"A chocolate malt. I will get skinny with this dang straw diet and I want to counteract that."

"Sorry. I don't have one for you. Maybe when you are stronger we'll get one. How's that?"

"If that's the best you can do, then that's the best you can do," I answered grinning with a half smile. I was too tired for a whole smile. Besides, my cheeks hurt.

"I think you should go to your room now and rest. This is your first day back and we don't want you getting over tired," Janet requested.

"What's this 'we' stuff?"

"Well, Manny, Barbara and myself, silly," she explained.

"Of course. Sorry. The clenched teeth give my words the wrong inflection."

Janet walked with me to my bedroom. I turned to look at her with questioning eyes.

"What's this?" I saw a small bed, next to my double sized bed.

"We thought it best you have an adjustable bed because you can't lie flat."

"Oh my. You're right. I expected to see lots of pillows to prop me up."

"No, this is better."

"Well, thanks. How do I pay for it?"

"All taken care of. Your kids insisted. And, your daughter will be here by tonight and will stay with you until you are strong enough to be on your own."

"Cool," was all I could manage, not being able to express my gratefulness for all the care and support they offered.

Manny and Barbara went to the airport to get my daughter, and when I woke up, she was in a chair by my bed and informed me that Janet cleaned up the kitchen, left more soup, and had gone back to her place.

***

A week went by fast as I recovered my strength with help from my friends and my daughter. We walked several times a day and soon I could do it on my own.

We had a long and heartfelt hug the day my daughter left to return to her home. Some people's kids are great. The first day alone was scary. I had to prepare my foods and make sure they were sloppy enough to get through the straw. There are all kinds of things that can be liquefied, and I bought vitamins and prescriptions in that form. Hiding the taste of those with vanilla flavored shakes became a necessity. The sucking and swallowing method is tiring. You use muscles you didn't know you had. I wondered how it would feel to chew my food again.

Janet and Manny visited daily and we had much to discuss.

"The authorities found Mary," Manny announced one afternoon.

"Really. That's wonderful. How did you find out?" I asked.

"I called the Sheriff's Department, and they filled me in. When they found Damon, at the house where we saw his truck, they arrested him for assault and battery, you know, for what he did to you. That's where Mary was. After they questioned him, sounded like it took several hours, Damon gave them the information they needed to find her. I bet the car that zoomed out of there took her to another location. Anyway, it's my understanding they found her the day after Damon slugged you.

"Holy cow! Is she okay?" I asked.

Manny sighed before he spoke again. "I don't know. No one's seen her back at her apartment, and of course, the deputies wouldn't tell me anything about her whereabouts, only that she is safe, whatever that means."

"Safe could mean she is no longer in danger. My guess is she's staying somewhere to recoup. I am not aware of any relatives that live nearby. We'll have to wait it out, once again," I said.

I did my best not to worry about Mary. I felt certain she would return to our complex eventually.

I went to coffee one morning, even though I couldn't drink it hot. Martha helped me out and produced a cold cup for me flavored with chocolate and almond. I opened the drawers in the community kitchen area and found an unused straw.

"You're looking mighty peaked these days, Dee," she scolded as she frowned.

"I do my best to scare you," I answered. I'm not positive she thought I was joking.

"Well, it's up to you to take care of yourself, you know. No one here is up to doing it for you," she admonished.

"This will pass, Martha. It takes time."

The ten people seated at the table jumped up out of their seats, startling me. I stood up too, wondering what had happened.

"Oh my gosh," one shouted.

"Get the spray," another yelled.

When I saw the air freshener in someone's hand, I beat it for the door. If I coughed from the spray, I'd be in big trouble.

I stood outside the door, watching the small chaotic dance the few residents inside were doing. Ten minutes later, one of them joined me outside.

"What in the heck is going on?" I asked.

"Oh, you know, Marten Gilbert. The one who brags about the crap he eats. He blew a 7.0 on the fart scale."

"Oh. Egad. Glad I left the room."

"Ya. Especially in your condition," she said.

"Guess I hadn't thought of it as a condition. Interesting," I said.

The woman looked at me as if she couldn't remember what she just said. "So, Dee, where is your friend Mary these days? Somebody told me she packed up and left. Was she mad at you because you took up with Damon?"

"Oh dear. No, no, no," I said, shaking my head. "Mary needed medical attention and she'll be back when she's better. And, you must listen to me carefully. I did not, 'take up with Damon' as you put it. He is not a friend of mine. I have not, and will not, ever have anything to do with Damon," I explained and this time I thought my clenched teeth were an advantage in getting my point across.

"I'm sorry. I must have misunderstood what someone told me. But, no, come to think of it, that's what I heard. Someone else has the wrong information," she added.

"Please don't give out any more bad information," I said.

"I am really sorry. No, if the subject comes up, I'll straighten them out," she said.

"Thank you. I must be on my way. See you later," I said, knowing if she couldn't remember who told her there was little chance she would correct the information.

I walked back to my apartment hoping I'd impressed some truth into the woman's memory, and passed a group of four, out walking their dogs. I smiled and said hello and they greeted me with pleasant comments. They made me realize I only had to deal with a broken jaw. Two of those lovely women because of curvatures in their spines, are bent forward and I'm certain it is a permanent condition. I've noticed that older people, when they have knees or hips replaced, get around with walkers for months. In order to grip the handles, you have to bend forward. I think if you are in that position for too long a time, you will end up staying that way. Someone should invent a better design for those contraptions. Their daily lives must be difficult, uncomfortable, and I don't know what else.

My thoughts turned to Mary. I phoned the Sheriff's office several times to inquire, but they wouldn't give me any information because I am not family or related in any way.

I made a trip to the Sheriff's main office. I was ushered into the main office. The newly elected Sheriff was kind enough to see me.

"I am sorry I cannot answer your questions, Ms. Anderson. Her whereabouts must remain confidential until she decides to make contact with you. I can assure you she is doing well and will be back in her apartment soon," he told me.

"Why is it confidential?" I asked.

This man, who had replaced his older predecessor and was a great deal better looking, pursed his lips as if he was not happy with my question. "I can't give you any further details, but I appreciate your concern." He stood up and indicated the question and answer session was finished.

I thanked him for seeing me, and he told me to call anytime I had any further questions and his department would do their best to give me answers.

It is frustrating not to have any new information about Mary. In my head I have imagined all sorts of things that could have happened to her. She could be hospitalized with injuries or wounds. Or in a mental hospital recovering from trauma. Or, heaven forbid, she went back to her home state to stay with, well, I don't know. I am not familiar with who her friends might be back there. Still no word from her, and each time I walk by her place, the drapes remain closed tight against the hot summer sun and shutting out the world and the people who care about her.

CHAPTER TWENTY-THREE

Morning coffee and monthly birthday parties are a great venue to bring people together and to meet new residents. The old high school type of clicks remain intact, however. Some save seats for their friends and newbees often are left alone to fend for themselves. You must be assertive if you wish to be included. I began to go to morning coffee more often, seeking the company of anybody to replace Mary's absence. That proved to be a mistake that caused me heartache.

Geraldine, I call her Ms. Runnamouth, is a gossip who believes she is giving out information everyone wants to know. At least every other day she gives updates on resident's whereabouts and assignations. Her keen eyes saw Mary's meetings with Damon and she states exactly what she thinks she sees and what others do. No lies there, but she is spreading other people's information, actions and conditions without their consent. Her thinly veiled remarks about Damon and possible paramours left no doubt she's referring to Mary without naming her. I felt pain for Mary's implied involvement. My guess is Runnamouth would have spoken her name if I hadn't been there. I am embarrassed for Mary and my comment was too little, too late.

"We don't have any business spreading rumors about people's private lives, Geraldine. It makes me wonder if you aren't trying to deflect scrutiny on your own private life," I said.

Geraldine passed by that statement without a pause, moved on to tell us how so-and-so moved out of her lover's rental, and begged to get back with her husband.

The coffee drinkers were uncomfortable with my statement and were happy to pounce on a new topic. Then the discussion turned to the bus's ever changing schedule. Drivers are difficult to find and the complex's owner's, in their quest to make money, must keep their expenses out of the negative column.

I left soon afterward and decided to return to the table less often.

Tilly is on my mind today. I use my cell phone to call her.

"Tilly, are you home right now?" I asked.

"Yes, dear. Otherwise, I couldn't answer your call. I don't have any of those new fangled gadgets, you know," she answered.

"I would like to come over, is that okay?" I asked.

"Would you do me a big favor and come over this afternoon? I want you to see something," she asked.

"Okay. I can do that. I'll see you then," I responded.

"Oh, and bring your binoculars, please," she added.

I told her I would, wondering why I would need them. I thought about it and decided she must be worried about the young people using the pool at night. Residents are concerned they are not visiting relatives in the complex.

I made my way over to Tilly's building and climbed the fifteen stairs up to her front door.

Tilly greeted me with her usual sweet smile.

"Come in, sweetie. Thank you for coming," she said.

"How in the heck do you get your groceries up here?"

"Very carefully. I get a ride two times a week when the bus isn't running, so I don't have much to carry each time I shop."

"Good plan, Tilly."

"Now come and join me on the patio. Would you like some iced tea?"

"Sure. No sweetener, though. And Tilly, I have to have a straw with it."

Tilly returned with a tray that jiggled as she walked and I watched the overfilled glasses spill liquid on the tray.

"Here we are. Now drink up and relax. The show will begin soon," she said.

"Show?"

"You just wait. It will be interesting and just as I said."

We talked of unimportant matters and she inquired about my jaw.

"Give me the binoculars, please," she requested.

She held them up to her eyes and used the adjustments. "There. Right there. Now you look exactly over there, that palm tree right above the office building," she instructed.

I adjusted the glasses for my vision. "Oh my. What the heck is that?"

"See? I keep telling everyone. There's someone up there."

"I think you are right, Tilly. What in the world is he doing?"

"He makes a nest or something. Out of the dead palm leaves. I think he might sleep there at night."

"You think?" I continued to watch the movements in the tree. Soon it seemed like a basket of sorts was swaying. "Can you see that without the binoculars?" I asked.

"You bet I can. I've been watching for months."

The next thing I noticed was alarming. "Oh my god. There's a fire in that palm."

I put the glasses down. "Tilly, lookit." I was aghast.

Both of us jumped up when we heard a loud cry of "Whoohoo."

A rounded mass of dead palms shot down to the ground, burning with wisps of smoke rising above it.

"Tilly where's your fire extinguisher."

"In the kitchen under the sink."

"Call 911," I yelled as went to the kitchen.

I pulled the cylinder from the cupboard and ran out her front door. "You wait here," I shouted.

As soon as I came close to the tree, I pulled the pin and squeezed the trigger, moving the nozzle back and forth over the flames that crept higher and higher. The pile was big. The cylinder felt heavy and I wondered if I would be able to extinguish the flames. I looked up, wondering how the fire got started. Was there really a man up there as Tilly had told us?" Someone hollered 'whoohoo', but I can't see anyone up there. I kept moving the extinguisher back and forth, as I considered the possibility.

The fire truck came and had the mass under control immediately. Then they asked how it happened.

"Well, sir, someone lit a bunch of dead palm leaves on fire and it came crashing down. My neighbor claims someone has been living up there, or at least spending time up there," I explained.

They looked at me as if I had some screws loose.

"No, really," I said.

I'm not sure how the next things happened because my adrenalin was no longer giving me the energy I needed. A sheriff's car arrived, and they asked me to repeat what I'd told the firemen. They looked up the palm tree and shouted instructions several times. I was astounded to see a skinny little man shinny down the trunk.

I heard Tilly's little feet pattering up the sidewalk and she stood next to me, watching the man come down the tree.

"See? I told you. That's what I've been seeing for a long time."

"Ya, Tilly. You were right. I wouldn't have believed it if I hadn't seen it myself."

"We hung around hoping for an explanation. After a while, one fireman explained that the man is a homeless person who seems to be a little off mentally, and someone would find a better place for him to stay."

"Oh good. Poor man. What an imagination he has, though. Think about that. Who would decide to live up in a palm tree at night and make it work?" Tilly said.

"Tilly, we've had a lot of excitement today. Let's get out of here."

"I just knew someone was up there. All those people who didn't believe me. Now I've got a story to tell, don't I?"

"It's beyond me why anyone, mentally ill or what have you, would choose a palm tree to perch in for any length of time. Let's go back to your patio and finish our tea. I'm exhausted," I suggested.

I think I shook my head for another hour, wondering why in heck a person would do what that little man did.

***

After six weeks, the bands came off my molars. Everything healed according to my doctors.

On this day in late October, I remained on my patio for several minutes. The outside temperature was cool enough to enjoy my coffee. This time I drank it from a cup without a straw. It felt wonderful and tasted better than anything I'd drank in a long while.

I noticed a car coming in the gate. A person resembling a female in the passenger seat was looking up in my direction. Something was familiar, but from that distance, I could have imagined it.

CHAPTER TWENTY-FOUR

The next morning I woke up to my cell phone ringing. I didn't recognize the number of the caller and didn't answer. The bing I heard showed there was a voicemail message. I put in my code and listened. It was Mary, asking me to call her. I returned the call right away.

Mary's voice sounded hesitant. "Hello, Dee, is this you?"

"Yes. I am so happy to hear from you. You must have changed your number. I didn't recognize it so I didn't answer."

"Yes, I did get a new number. And a new phone, too. Anyway, I am calling because, well, I know I have a lot of explaining to do. Tell me when you are available to talk. I'd prefer you come to my place."

"Of course I'll come. Is later this morning okay?"

"Yes. Just you, though, Dee."

"I understand. Should I text you before I come over?"

"Thank you. That would be best."

I was in and out of the shower faster than the time it took Damon to break my jaw. I doused myself with all the oil and cream necessary to protect my Midwestern skin from the intense Arizona sun, brushed on the minimum amount of makeup to look presentable, selected what I wore yesterday, since I hadn't bothered to hang it up and prepared to go to Mary's. I have to prepare myself for a meeting like this. My heart is beating faster than usual, anticipating what she might tell me, and, well, I'm not a young chickie anymore and I have work to do to get in better physical shape. The jaw deal set me back in that department.

I texted Mary to let her know I was on my way.

The door opened revealing a thin person I found the sight of, difficult to comprehend.

"Come in, Dee." Mary walked into her dining area.

"I've made coffee. Would you like some?" she asked.

"Only if I can give you a hug, first."

Mary hesitated and then moved closer. I hugged her with gentle pressure. She felt frail and I noticed her eyes were tearing up. She held me close for several seconds.

"I'm not sure I can apologize enough to you, Dee, and I feel awful, the way I talked to you."

When I released my slight hold on her, I looked into her eyes. "You must have had a reason. I would guess I overstepped my bounds, asking for explanations you were not prepared to give."

"There was no way I could explain anything to you then, Dee. I was in trouble and I'd found information that threw me into a situation I didn't know how to handle."

"Apology accepted, then. You may confide in me or not, your choice."

"I want to tell you what happened to me. I'll get the coffee," she said. She brought the electric pot to the table with a plate of croissants and a dish of blueberry jam.

"Yum. My favorite. Thank you."

"I remember."

"Are you doing okay, Mary? Do you need help with anything? You look thinner than when I last saw you."

"I've had a difficult time eating enough to gain back the weight I lost," she admitted. "It will take a while before I'm ready to get out and see others, so I'll need patience. Time and a sympathetic ear, I think will be most helpful and I need your assistance getting this place cleaned up. It's been sitting here getting dusty and well, when they slapped me around there were bloodstains left that need to be washed out. I have tried, but I wasn't successful getting rid of it."

"I'll do whatever you need." I took a bite of the roll with a large dollop of jam. "You'll have to tell me when you want me to begin. We could both use a couple of rounds of malts, don't you think?"

"For sure. You've lost weight, too. You look a hell of a lot better than I do. I understand Damon broke your jaw. It's my fault he came after you. I am so sorry," Mary said.

"No need to apologize, Mary. He did it, not you. Besides, he caught me in here snooping around. I had no real business doing it except I hoped I would find something that would help me find you. Can you tell me anything about where you were or who hurt you? Or is it too soon to ask?"

"It's okay, Dee." Mary turned her head toward the front door and then focused again on me.

"I've been in a drug rehabilitation facility."

"Serious?"

"I was feeling lousy for a while. Damon was giving me stuff he said would make me feel better. I didn't have any idea he was giving me narcotics. Of course, I got hooked."

"Oh. That's not good. Do you know what they were?"

"I was told it was Valium," she answered. "Made me groggy and my surroundings looked blurry nearly all the time.

"You must have been disoriented most of the time."

"I was. Every now and then I'd have some clarity, but not often."

"Gosh. So it takes a while to stop being addicted?"

"Well. I'm not sure you are ever not addicted, but you can stop using. I'm in pretty good shape right now. It'll still take some work."

"Well, if there's ever a time you need me, to talk, or just sit with you, if that's what it takes, I'd be happy to help."

"Thanks, Dee. I appreciate your concern. I may take you up on that."

"I have to ask, how did you find Damon attractive enough to date? I never imagined he'd be on your wish list."

"I wouldn't exactly call it dating. This might shock you Dee. It was just about sex. I needed a man in my life. I guess I didn't care at that point who. He was convenient and exceptional, Dee. I've never experienced such complete sexual fulfillment."

"No, I'm not shocked, Mary. Bewildered is more like it. Women have desires, some more than others. Maybe it would have been better if you had tried the speed-dating route like Janet and I did. We weren't successful at finding anyone, but you might have been. He didn't meet your emotional needs, I take it."

"No. All he ever talked about was himself and what he wanted. He told me about things he did and he was always the hero. Saving everybody. His mother, his sister, even his wife. I cannot imagine how he could have 'saved' her. She is a lovely, independent woman. He saw me as someone to rescue, I think. The more I saw him, the more controlling and mean he became. I tried to break it off and that's when he threatened me. I learned later what those threats entailed. At the end, he was punching and slapping me."

My mind flashed back to the day I took her by the arm and she winced.

"I wondered about that because you were acting strange the day you were angry with me and when I took your arm you looked as if I'd caused you pain. I am so mad he hurt you, Mary. What an awful thing to go through. Did it happen often?"

"Often enough. He always hit me in places that my clothes would cover up. Methodical hurting, I'd call it."

I shook my head in disbelief. "I feel even worse that you felt you couldn't come to me and tell me of your situation. I must say or do something that made you feel you couldn't trust me or confide in me."

"No, Dee. My pride got in the way in addition to the fact that down deep, I thought I was being pretty stupid to resort to having sex with someone like Damon. Who'd want to admit to that?"

"Well, it's so much junk in the dumper, I say. Good riddance. He's behind bars. I hope it is for a long, long time."

"So, was it Damon who kidnapped you?"

"No. You better have another cup of coffee, Dee. It's a long, complicated story."

She poured and I ate another croissant and listened.

"There is a group of people that call themselves the TCOA, The Coalition of Americans. I've been told it is a small group with few members. One of them took me out of here. Their purpose is to rid the United States of relatives of Germans, no matter the number of generations forward they have to go. Damon was in the group. I would call him an enforcer."

"Why would he mess with you, then?"

"They believe the Nazi manifesto is taught and passed down, generation to generation of Germans in the belief that one day those who are indoctrinated will rise and swell to a force that will dominate the world once again. My grandmother on my mother's side was living in France at the time of the occupation by the German army. She waited on tables at an entertainment facility and sometimes danced with officers. I have little information about her activities. She may have been intimate with some officers. I don't care. Point is, there are photographs of her being dragged through the streets of France exhibited as a traitor after the Germans left the town where she lived. They shaved the women's hair to brand them."

"I saw the picture in the notebook," I said.

"You have it? I looked everywhere for it. No wonder I couldn't find it."

"So, you being a great granddaughter made you a candidate for this TCOA group to find?"

"Yes, that's what I am told."

"That's sick. Not sick, terrific as the kids say today. Do you know, is it a large group, nationwide, or what?" I asked.

"My information is that it is in its infancy with a core group here in Daystar City and other small sects in major cities. I doubt there are more than four of them here, all men, except one. Those men, all of them, are facing charges of kidnapping and murder. I'll be giving testimony at their trials."

"Murder? Who was killed?"

Mary waited a few seconds before speaking again. She did not answer my question.

"The Sheriff's deputy told me Manny gave information that led to the authorities finding me. Do you know anything about that, Dee?"

"Yes, I do. He thought he knew the area where that driver took us the day we went on the Daystar City Tour and I asked him to take me there. Barbara went with us. Manny spotted Damon's truck parked in front of a house. He and I went snooping. I peeked in the window."

"See anything?"

"Yes. There were two women on a couch, and two, or maybe three men, yelling about something. I couldn't make out any words. The women had big scarves or some such over their faces."

"No kidding. That was you. One of them thought he saw something by the window and went to look. They were more than a little upset. You were lucky not to get caught."

"What happened to you after they went to the window?"

"We were rushed out of there. Being blindfolded, I didn't know where to, but it felt like we went to a garage. They put me in one of their cars and the driver drove lickety-split out of there. With no reference points, I couldn't get any idea of my location.

"What about the other woman I saw sitting next to you on the couch? It was you, right? Do you know her?"

"I'm sure it was Kathleen. You remember, the woman who wears such bright colored clothes. Anyway, it sounded like her. She bitched the whole time. They slapped her around more than me. I got the idea she was with them in the beginning and she must have turned against them. At first, she talked to me about my heritage and how important it is to know your lineage. If you had German blood, she said it was better to end your life to stop the Nazi radicalization of relatives of American Citizens and all Americans."

"That's terrible. How'd she get on their bad side?"

"I don't know for sure. One day there was a lot of arguing between them. From then on, they ordered her to keep quiet and stay by me. I heard her whimpering too. I think they beat her."

"Did they beat you?"

"No. A few slaps here and there. They used drugs to control me. The feelings it gave me seemed similar to the stuff Damon gave me. I felt relaxed, most of the time. Didn't have the gumption to fight back or argue or try to get out of the situation."

"No wonder you needed treatment. That's awful. I'm so sorry you went through that."

"Dee, I'm doing okay. I don't have a physiological dependency. And I have made a lot of improvement. I am getting good counseling and I'll continue with it for awhile."

"So, it wasn't Jane with you, then."

"No. Did you think it might be? Maybe it is best left alone."

"Why would that be? You know something?"

"It's something I feel. I can't explain it."

"Okay. I'll go with that."

"Well, I still haven't figured out her disappearance. So, it could have been this same group that killed Jane. Do you think that's possible? I was confused about her son's location and possible involvement in her death. I believe you tried to get us off his track when you first said you found him in New York, and the next time he was mentioned, you said he was in LA," I said.

"I was not thinking straight. I don't remember saying that," Mary said.

"Dee, I need to get some things off my chest. I've learned a great deal about myself in the past months. I was jealous of Janet and her money, even jealous of you and your self-confidence. I didn't feel worthy of either of your friendships."

"Oh, gosh. I'm sorry to hear that from you. I must not have let you know how much having you as a friend meant to me," I said.

"You probably did tell me. I just didn't hear it. I wanted more money, and I didn't care how I got it. Damon had me convinced he could save me from my meager lifestyle. I was tired of shopping in thrift stores and constantly looking for discounted meats and groceries. I wanted to be able to go out and buy new clothes whenever I wanted. I wanted to go to expensive restaurants and not worry about the cost."

"Do you still feel that way?" I asked.

"No. Well, most of the time I don't. I'm getting better at accepting what I have. Who I am. I am solvent and I am learning to appreciate different things," she answered. "I made terrible decisions and became very selfish. I regret all that."

"I am happy you have started a new beginning. Please, say what is on your mind if I get overbearing or too pushy," I suggested.

"Best I can do is try. As I said, I need patience and time. I am ashamed of my conduct and it may take some time to work past it," Mary said.

You look tired, Mary. Do you want to rest?"

"Yes, but will you come back this afternoon and help with cleaning?"

"Sure. I'll do that." I put my plate and coffee cup in the kitchen sink. A quick look around and I could see some tasks awaiting my efforts.

I left Mary's and went back to my place. To think Kathleen took up with those kinds of people. She must have gone after Jane somehow. I'll bet she was in on her disappearance. Mary thinks it best to leave that alone. Now, why would that be? She confessed so much to me today. I didn't want to push for any more information. It has to be hard to own up to such things. She said she needs time. So,

I guess I have to give her that. Getting info about who was murdered. Not going to leave that alone. Not gonna do it.

Chapter Twenty-Five

After I left Mary I got my mail and headed into the community room. I hoped to see Manny or Barbara. They often played Bingo on this day.

The games hadn't begun and I got Barbara's attention.

"I've just talked with Mary. I wanted to let you know."

"Is she okay?"

"Yes, but she's not up to socializing yet."

"Thanks. I'll tell Manny."

Janet never plays Bingo, so I didn't expect to see her there. The games commenced and the familiar sounds began.

The Terminator was drawing the numbers. She acknowledged my presence with a nod. "B-6." The sea of gray and white-headed players bowed toward the tables, followed by daubers marking cards in unison, singing the rhythmic song of possible winnings. Pum, pum, pum, pum, pum. Their uppermost bodies rise and wait for the next number.

"G-60," again, heads down, pum, pum, pum, pum, pum. The sounds echo out as if to signal to the great Bingo players in the sky that soon, their numbers will come up.

I turned to watch as participants bowed their heads toward the table once again and put stains on the numbered squares. I laughed to myself because it looked and sounded funny. As I exited the room, I reminded myself they were having a great time.

The sounds of the passing freight train, whoot-whooting its way through our city assaulted my eardrums when I stepped outside. As I walked further down the sidewalk, the planes from the nearby air force base roared their path through the skies. I don't mind their noise, but the trains irk me. It's a fact that most senior housing is built in areas where land is the least expensive and to hell with the noise factors. I think developers believe we are all deaf and it shouldn't matter to us. They are deaf to our need for peace and quiet in our advancing years.

I walked around the grounds of the complex and sat on a cement bench in an area with flowering bushes, referred to as Ponder Point. The nearby trees and palms offered protection from the sun. I have several ideas to consider.

Mary has not divulged pertinent information regarding Jane and her disappearance. Where she disappeared to, and if she is dead are questions that remain. I will need to see those documents in that manila envelope again. When I first got a quick look at it I didn't read everything and my memory became clouded after my encounter with Damon. The notebook might confirm some of my suspicions. I'll go over it again before I give it back.

I reached home in a state of inattention to my surroundings. My neighbor greeted me as she went out her door. I grunted an acknowledgement, fumbling for my keys, deep in thought.

A short nap would reenergize me. Forty-five minutes later I rose from my lounge chair feeling rested. I freshened myself at the vanity and returned to the chair, notebook in hand.

I decided that could wait. I went to my computer and put the copied disc I'd made from the office's computer in the slot.

After an hour of searching, I finally isolated the date Jane left her apartment with a man. The pictures were grainy and worse when I enlarged them. I zeroed in on her clothing, the man's clothing, and their faces. Their body language suggested they were comfortable with one another, because there was no trace of fear in her face or body language. The man's face was difficult to bring into focus. I stared at it anyway. It didn't resemble the face I recalled from the grocery store after all. I didn't have a clue as to his identity.

I flipped past the pictures in the notebook. Further into the scrambled information a handwritten accounting lent clarity to Jane's Grandmother's living situation. She worked as a housekeeper to a wealthy family before she married. Her early life, living in France during World War II, was filled with work and volunteering at the local social club. There was no information in her writings beyond her early life. The next notations contained warnings forbidding discussion about circumstances specific to family movements and whereabouts.

Jane's notes about herself recounted a somber home life, a father who was absent most of the time, and a mother whose life revolved around keeping food on the table. There was no mention of other siblings.

The notebook allowed me to see how Jane, because of her lonely and uninteresting childhood, with a father who was absent most of her life, sought to find better living circumstances. Her notes indicated she became involved with several different men, but found something she needed in the man she stayed with those years in Chicago. The clipping about his death coupled with the pictures made me believe she had something to hide.

I closed the notebook and then noticed a paper tucked into a pocket on the back cover, folded in half. I opened it. There was a date and a note to herself to get her DNA analyzed.

I remembered those were the kind of results in the manila envelope I'd found at Mary's. There were other papers also, and I think I saw two birth certificates. One must have been Mary's and maybe the other belonged to her Mother.

I put the notebook, along with my keys, cellphone, and sunglasses on the raised kitchen counter while I looked for my cat so I could feed him before I left for Mary's. He was playing 'Let's Make A Deal', hiding behind curtain number two in the living room. I interrupted his fantasies and he seemed more interested in playing than in my verbal offer of food, so I spent a half-hour tossing the string with a toy on the end for him to capture.

Play ended when he plopped down on the carpet, breathing hard. I filled his food bowl and then texted Mary. She agreed this was a good time for me to come over.

We vacuumed and dusted and I worked on getting the bloodstains out of her sheets. When I took them out of the dryer, there were grayish areas remaining.

"These don't look too hot. Besides, every time you put these on your bed, it will remind you how they got there. I think you should buy a new set," I said.

"It's not in my budget, Dee."

"Forget the budget for now. Let me fire up your computer and I'll order a set. What color you would like?" I asked.

"You want me to pay you back?"

"No, I don't. I've wondered what nice little thing I could do for you, and here it is," I answered.

"Like helping me clean isn't enough?"

Mary returned with her laptop and I ordered a set of sheets, lilac in color.

"You want lilac smelly stuff to go with them?" I asked.

Mary smiled for the first time that afternoon. "That would be wonderful. You are very kind."

"Okay, that's done. Should be here next Monday. Now what do we need to do?"

"I'll get us some iced tea. I'm parched."

Mary returned with two tall glasses filled with amber liquid, lots of ice cubes, and a slice of lemon perched on the rims.

Mary turned on the TV to the four o'clock news to watch as we sipped the refreshing drink.

The newscaster spoke in concerned and animated tones as he announced breaking news unfolding in Tucson. "An hour ago, a man and women were found dead in their home."

The camera then focused on a reporter at the scene. "This is a suspected murder/suicide situation. The names of the victims will not be released until next of kin are notified."

"Dee. You are as white as a bleached dishtowel. Are those people you know?" she asked.

"I sure hope not." I felt apprehensive.

My phone rang. I picked it up and answered it. I listened with my eyes closed. My heart sank.

"Dee, what is it?"

"That was Janet. The couple in Tucson is her brother and his wife."

"Oh no. What did she say?"

"She's on her way down there now, so she doesn't know how or what happened."

"Oh dear. What can we do to support her?" Mary asked.

"We'll figure that out later, after she learns what happened," I answered.

We finished drinking our tea in silence. My thoughts were with Janet.

Later that afternoon, Janet called. She sounded distraught.

"The coroner determined my brother died at least twenty-four hours before his wife. They found him on the living room couch. He'd been hit on the head with a baseball bat."

"Janet, I am stunned. So she didn't shoot him."

"No. I never did get her gun back to her. Couldn't do it."

"How did she die, then," I asked.

"I figure, and the detective they assigned agreed, that she probably got up the next day, found him dead, and in her confusion or grief decided to kill herself. She had a ton of barbiturates in her system."

"That is so sad. I am so sorry for your loss Janet. Is there anything I can do to help you?" I asked.

"No. I will get a cleaning company to come in and clean the place up. Then I'll decide what to do with their belongings. I talked to their neighbors. They told me there have been loud arguments for several days this week. Once, they called the police, but they don't know how things were resolved. Neighbors didn't hear anything today because they were out shopping when it happened. It was the mail carrier, who noticed their mail hadn't been picked up for a couple of days who called the authorities."

"Amazing he even noticed."

"Guess he knew them, you know, from delivering mail, they had pleasant conversations over the years."

"Where are you staying?"

"I found a quaint motel not too far from their place. It'll do me until I have the situation under control. I am going to plan a small memorial service for them and invite neighbors. Don't feel you have to make the trip, Dee. It's too far on those awful freeways."

"We'll keep you in our thoughts, Janet."

"We?"

"Mary is back and I'm helping her with a few things. I was at her place when we heard the news on the TV."

"Is she okay?"

"Yes, and she seems like she's on the way back to being the gal we both know and love."

"Oh, good. Well, listen. I won't keep you any longer. I'll stay in touch."

"Please call, even if you just need someone to listen, okay?"

"Sure. Bye, Dee."

I felt drained after hearing about Mary's challenges earlier and then Janet's situation. Knowing I can't change those circumstances, I can only offer sympathy for Janet and Mary's needs. Janet is a methodical person. She will deal with her brother's death in an organized way, planning the memorial, and putting their home in order. My guess is she will sell it. I wondered if she was the heir. Mary needs my time, to listen and to make her place presentable again. Today will not see me doing any more physical work.

Chapter Twenty-Six

The weekend passed as slow as mud and sand layering to form a rock. I napped twice on Saturday and no phone calls interrupted my rest. On Sunday, I washed clothes and put them away ignoring the items that needed pressing. Sunday evening Janet called with details regarding her brother's memorial.

"I liked how you planned your Mom's, so I did something similar. More neighbors showed up than I expected. Guess they found good friends throughout the years," Janet said.

"Were you able to arrange home cleaners?"

"Yes. They did a fabulous job. The house looks great."

"Did you find a realtor?"

"No, Dee. I am seriously considering staying here. I found their will, and they left everything to me. They didn't have children and I don't think she was close to anyone in her family. Actually, now that I think about it, she was an only child and her parents passed away five years ago," Janet explained.

"Staying there? Wow. That is a big change for you."

"There's a pool in the backyard, which needs major grooming and I think I'll update the kitchen too. The area is lovely and far enough from the malls to keep the neighborhood quiet."

"Good for you. Lots of challenges and forward-looking prospects. I'll miss you terribly."

"I'll miss you too, but you might want to think about taking a bus down here to visit. A pool to ourselves. How about that?"

"You sound positive and upbeat. I wondered how you would handle all of this."

"I won't go into how sad and guilty I feel. I can't change what happened."

"I doubt you could have done anything to prevent it, Janet."

"I know, but I can't help but feel I should have done something. Now I'm focusing on restructuring my life now that my Arizona anchors are gone. It's kept my mind from thinking too much about their deaths. His wife would die eventually, after a difficult time, maybe years. That would have been hard for my brother because he was loyal and loving with her. Now he's spared from it. Not what you would wish for, of course. It does give me some comfort to know he won't have to go through such trying times,"

"I can understand those feelings. I am happy to hear how you are forging ahead. The sadness will hit you when you least expect it, Janet. Let it happen. Tears and heartache have a way of clearing the forest of thoughts and emotions from unnecessary brush."

"Well, that is a lovely thought. Thank you," Janet paused and took a long breath.

"I must get going. I have thank you notes to write. And, before I forget, thank you for the sculpture of the brother and sister. It is beautiful and was so thoughtful of you. I already called Mary to thank her too. By the way, she sounds like she's doing well, thanks to you."

"I think so too. You are welcome for the gift, Janet. Do take care and stay in touch. I'll think about that bus trip."

***

That night around nine-thirty the fire alarms went off. I was dressed in my pajamas, so I grabbed a robe, my purse, cellphone, and keys. My cat was already under the bed. I went out into the alcove and took the five flights of stairs down to the bottom floor. I saw people were already out there.

"Anybody know what happened? Is there a fire in the building?" I asked.

"Don't know. No one is telling us anything," someone answered.

"I don't smell smoke, do you?" I asked.

"No. Must be something else caused the emergency,"

"Yes, but the fire alarms went off," I said.

"No telling what it is," one of the men answered.

An hour passed. Standing on cement is uncomfortable to say the least. I decided to go sit in my car.

Fifteen minutes later, I noticed a fireman talking to the residents. I got out of my car and joined them.

"What's he saying?" I asked.

"Apparently one of the residents pulled the alarm. There's no fire in this building," one of the women told me.

"Hmm." I sighed. "I do wish we could stop meeting like this," I said.

A few folks chuckled.

I saw Dar standing a few yards down from me and I walked over to join her.

"Did you hear anything, Dar? Any idea what the emergency was?" I asked.

"Ya. Marten Gilbert, you remember him? The one who eats such terrible things? He's lost it, Dar. His memory is shot. He lives next door to me, you know. He came down the hall and banged on my door. He was distraught. I asked him what was the matter. He asked me to come and look at something in his apartment, so I did. I asked him again what was going on. He says, 'there's a stranger in here, and now I can't find him. You gotta help me.' He took me to the bedroom and stood in front of his dresser and pointed to the mirror. 'See,' he says. 'There he is again. Help me get him out of here'.

"Oh dear," I said.

"I mean, Dee, he was serious and panicky. I told him I would take care of it and I sent him to the living room. While he was in there, I took a sheet from the closet and hung it over the mirror. Then I told him not to worry, I took care of everything," Dar said.

"Oh. That is so sad. Well then, is he the one who pulled the fire alarm?"

"I think so. The firemen said the sheet was down when they went in and Marten was going on about the stranger, how he got scared and went out in the hall and pulled the alarm," she explained.

"So now what," I asked.

"I think the manager is trying to contact his granddaughter. Somebody's going to have to calm him down," Dar said.

I left Dar's side, went back to the sidewalk by the elevator, and waited for them to be up and running again, or an all clear to go back into our homes.

"Did Dar tell you what happened?" someone asked me.

"We were just talking. Maybe we'll find out tomorrow," I said. I didn't feel right about explaining Marten's problem to anyone else.

We were given the all clear and returned to our separate abodes, relieved that nothing serious happened to the building.

***

Monday morning shone bright with sunshine and cloudless blue skies eager to please every desert dweller. I brought out the notebook once again. I put it on the counter intending to return it to Mary. Instead, I sat down and flipped through the pages again.

At least three different women wrote in it. I determined they are women because men are noted as husbands, boyfriends, sons, or persons they dated. Chronologically it is out of order as if each person made notes, left the next page blank and then someone else would continue. The next person filled the empty page and wrote several pages beyond those entries. Confusing, but I learned how their lives unfolded, including Jane's. Nothing new came from reading it again, and I returned it to the counter and I felt the manila envelope must be the key to new information.

I texted Mary I to let her know I was on my way to see her, stopping at my mailbox first. Martha, the voice tornado, was right behind me a few yards back. She was regaling a story to her walking companion.

"Oh, hi there, Dee," she said as she approached.

"Martha. Hey. Look at you. Love your outfit. New? And walking shoes to match. Wow," I said.

"Thanks. It was time to get rid of those danged shoes that closed with those sticky strips. Hated them. What's new with you? Haven't seen the likes of you in quite some time."

"Busy, I guess. Helping Mary some," I answered.

"Oh. She's back. How come she was gone so long?" Martha asked.

"She had a medical issue and it took a while," I answered.

"I heard Damon had something to do with it," she said.

"Oh?" I answered.

"And you. You had that, what was it? Oh, ya. A broken jaw. That Damon's doing too?" Martha asked.

"Everything happened so fast Martha," I answered.

"He's gone, ya know. For good. His wife never showed up here again, either. I'm betting that SOB got thrown in jail for stuff he did here, like exposing himself and chasing women."

"I'm sure management had their reasons, whatever they were. He wasn't one of my favorite people either, Martha."

"What's happened to your other friend, Janet? Haven't seen her around lately," Martha asked.

"She's at her brother's house in Tucson. I think she'll probably stay there," I answered.

"Oh. Too bad. Nice lady. Dressed high tag, if you know what I mean."

257

"She has good taste, yes. I hope to visit her sometime down the road. Well, Martha, I'm on my way to Mary's. I'll see you again, soon," I said as I retreated and went on my way.

She opened the door as I approached. She looked rested and happy to see me. I handed her the notebook.

"Oh, thanks for returning it. I am sure you realized as I did, that there wasn't a lot of helpful information in there," Mary remarked.

"Interesting though," I said.

Mary put the notebook down on the coffee table and went to the kitchen, returning with refreshments.

"Before we start, I heard the fire truck sirens last night. Do you know what happened?"

"Ya. Marten Gilbert was hallucinating. He thought there was a stranger in his apartment."

"Poor guy. Will someone be coming to take care of him?"

"I imagine the family will be informed, but I don't know anything else,"

"That is sad. Well, shall we begin?" she asked, handing me a glass of iced tea.

"You bet. Where first?"

"Let's take the drapes down and fluff the dust out of them in the dryer," she suggested.

"Okay."

The stepladder aided our task and after an hour and a half, we were putting them back in place.

"They smell fresh now. What a relief. Thanks for washing the windows before we put them back up."

"You're welcome. I could use a refill," I said, holding my glass out toward her.

"Be right back."

We took a break for fifteen minutes and started in again.

Mary and I sorted through closets she claimed were in need of decluttering. Then she suggested we tackle the china cabinet.

"You won't toss out anything from here, will you?" I asked.

"No. The shelves and dishes need dusting. That stuff gets into every corner," she explained.

As I emptied the contents, I put everything on the dining table. I pulled open the two drawers, finding cloth napkins and flowery ceramic holders for them. My attention went to the manila envelope underneath the silverware chest as I took it out.

"Mary, I think this envelope holds documents you'd want to look at," I said. "I glanced at them, the day I came in here, but I'm not sure what I saw. Do you mind telling me what is there?"

She came next to me and took the envelope from my hands. "Oh, ya." Mary walked to the sofa and sat down, taking out the envelope's contents.

"No, I don't mind telling you about these documents. Guess you might as well know what I know."

She pulled out the contents and placed them on her lap.

"This is my birth certificate, and this one belongs to a half-sister. My father left my mother when I was young. I didn't know he had a daughter with the other woman he married. My Mom never told me," Mary said.

"How did you get it? I thought you could only get your own, not other people's," I asked.

"When I was talking to Jane, before all this happened, she had her DNA tested. She gave me information about her father that made me wonder why I had similar information about mine. Then I got my DNA tested. The company that does the testing informed me that Jane was a match with me because we shared paternal

DNA. The birth certificates confirmed it, since my dad is listed as the father on both,"

"I'm amazed. Jane is, or was, your half-sister," I said.

"Yes. Once we confirmed it, I filled in gaps of information for her, and she did the same for me. Her life with my father was not great and she developed hard feelings toward him. She left home young and worked as a server until she found the man she lived with and had a son. They never married, although she was happy with him for a long time.

"Mary, is Jane alive?"

"I don't know what to tell you, Dee." Mary's eyes went to the ceiling and they rotated back and forth until she looked down again.

"What I have to tell you, is confidential. It can't ever be talked about again," she said.

Mary told me things that sounded as if they should be published in a crime story magazine.

"Holy crap. I most certainly will not share that with anyone, I assure you," I said when she finished.

Interesting and unexpected information had passed from Mary's lips into my brain. I left her apartment tired from the chores we'd done and full of questions about what could be next.

The rest of the week passed without incident. Everything at Mary's looked neat and clean and my help wasn't needed, at least not for a while.

***

Saturday morning I got up earlier than usual to vacuum and do my laundry. The clothes hamper wasn't full, so I went to coffee instead.

The table was full and the men were bringing in another table to set up more room for others. I sat down at the second table and soon it filled. There were fresh donuts in the kitchen area and the residents passed them around. I often wondered why management offered sweets instead of fruits and vegetables.

"It's the only time I eat sweets," Margaret offered.

"Me too," someone else piped in.

"I guess it's okay then," I said. However, both those women are overweight. I sure hope these donuts don't contribute to future ill health.

Cold silence filled the room like the smog that once filled the evening streets of London. I turned to my left and watched The Terminator approach the table.

"You!" she pointed to the woman sitting across from me. Marion looked up and her face turned red.

"You and your big mouth. I call Bingo just fine. You're just too deaf and dumb to hear me. Well, enjoy your games. I won't be joinin' ya anytime soon."

Several of the men pushed back their chairs looking as if they would go after her. The irritating sound of the chairs grating movement on the non-skid vinyl flooring got everyone's attention.

"Listen here, Johnson. You don't speak to anyone like that," one of the men said.

"I just did and I'll say any damned thing I please. You morons never appreciated all I did for you, anyways," she said.

"You are a bully and have disgraced yourself in front of all of us," another man said.

The Terminator moved in close to him with her fist in front of his face. "See how you like this up your nose," she said.

The tables moved forward as people got up to stop her from hitting the man. Several grabbed her arms but she wrestled herself from their grip.

I heard someone say to 'let her go'.

She heavy footed it out the side door and slammed it shut.

As soon as the door closed, Ron, the Manager came out of his office.

"I'm sorry about that. Ms. Johnson will not be on our management team any longer. You won't have to deal with her," he said.

One by one, each resident smiled and then they all clapped their hands together and there was a collective "whoo-hoo, the wicked witch is gone."

"Goodness. I didn't realize she was so disliked," I said.

"Oh, you don't know. If someone besides regular players were in the room, she called the Bingo numbers just fine. More often, she would turn her back to us and give out the numbers. If you asked her to repeat it or speak louder, she'd tell you how stupid you are, or you should get hearing aids."

"Gee. That's terrible. Guess you don't have to worry about that now. I wonder who will take her place," I asked.

"I heard they won't replace her. Someone will have to volunteer to do Bingo," Marion said.

"Oh, you knew they were going to let her go?"

"Well, that's what I heard."

"There are other activities, though," I said.

"We'll just have to see what happens." Marion raised her coffee cup and made a toast. "Here's to life without The Terminator."

The donuts and coffee tasted darned good after that confrontation.

Chapter Twenty-Seven

I felt it was time to entertain my friends. I called Barbara, Manny and Mary. Janet was in town to direct the movers in emptying her apartment, and she had the thrift store picking up the items she did not wish to keep.

Mary accepted my invitation. The thought crossed my mind she might bow out but she sounded eager to see everyone.

Janet arrived first, carrying a bottle of expensive red wine. Barbara and Manny brought a chocolate cake for dessert. The last person to ring my doorbell was Mary. She gave me a hug and handed me a dish.

"What do we have here?" I asked.

"Cashews," Mary answered.

"What a good idea. Thank you." I took the dish and placed it on the coffee table.

Manny was in the kitchen, looking for the bottle opener.

"Lower shelf on the left, Manny," I instructed.

Wine glasses in hand, and filled, Manny proposed a toast. "To the gals and myself of Winter Gardens. May we all see the next year in good health and without tragedy."

"Hey, hey," we said in unison.

"Mary, you are looking better than ever. Whatever it is you are doing, keep doing it," Manny professed.

"Why thank you, Manny. I am taking better care of myself," she answered.

Several minutes passed as we munched on the cashews and sipped the wine.

"Mary, I am curious how the authorities caught up with Damon. I understand there were others arrested besides Damon," Barbara asked.

"He was on the loose long enough to go after Dee. Manny's information led them to Damon. The others, well, this is interesting. They found cat hair on a shirt one kidnapper wore. He dumped the shirt in the garbage at the house where they kept me, and the authorities tested the DNA on the hairs and it matched Pepper's DNA. Lucky, because they didn't have other evidence to tie them to kidnapping me," Mary explained.

"Who's Pepper," Manny asked.

"My cat," Mary answered.

"Oh ya. I forgot. That is interesting. You know what? I heard Kathleen disappeared about the same time you did. Is it in any way connected?" Manny asked.

"Yes, it is Manny. She was in their little group and they killed her," Mary said. "I didn't know she was dead until I went in for more questioning."

"Oh my gosh," Barbara said.

"Mary, is Jane connected to all of this, by any chance?" Janet asked.

"I can't give you any answers on that, Janet. It is a mystery to all of us," Mary said.

"Huh. I thought for sure we'd find out. As far as she's concerned, I still maintain, no body, no crime," Janet said.

"On a different subject, Janet, how are you adjusting to life in Tucson?" Mary asked.

"I love the area, and I'm finding the neighborhood friendly. I'm learning to play bridge. Oh, and my pool, I had it refurbished. You guys should take the bus and come visit for a weekend. I have plenty of room for all of you," Janet answered.

We talked for another fifteen minutes until I smelled the chicken hot dish in the oven. I knew it was time to serve it.

"Let's eat," I announced.

After everyone carried in their dinner plates and utensils, I filled the dishwasher and we retired to the living room.

"I have something very important to tell all of you," Mary said.

All eyes were on Mary as she took out a package from under her chair and walked to my chair.

"Manny, as much help as you were in giving directions and details to the Sheriff's deputies, someone was overlooked for her importance in all of this," she began. "Dee, it was you that asked Manny to take you to find me. If you hadn't done that, it is possible no one would have discovered my location," Mary said.

"This paper, in this frame, honors your heroism. Without you, they would have killed me, I'm sure. I will forever be in your debt for risking your life. You did, you know. If they had seen you and recognized who was looking in the window, you'd have been a gonner. Judging by what they did to Kathleen and myself, I can say these are ruthless people, lacking in morals and decency. Their goal was to kill people of German descent and put others in their control. You saved me from that with your continued efforts to find me," she said.

"Are they all over the United States and have an organization name?" Janet asked.

Mary explained the purpose of the TCOA group. "There are few of them in our city and they are all going to prison for their deeds. You don't have to worry about more abductions. The authorities tell me it was mostly just talk and a way to frighten people," Mary said.

"Sick," Manny said. "And yes, Dee. You were the hero, not me."

I stood up and took the framed award from Mary and we hugged. Tears flowed from both of us.

"Okay, you two. That's enough," Janet interrupted. "Here's a tissue. Now, wipe up and let the rest of us in on the hug."

We weren't the only ones in need of a tissue. Janet, Barbara, and Manny wanted to get hold of the box and claim a tissue for their own eyes.

I suggested we each have a little more wine. I am told chocolate cake and wine go together and one must never avoid an opportunity.

The afternoon ended on a high note. The information Mary gave them satisfied their curiosity. I knew more facts, but revealing them would not serve any purpose.

***

Weeks later, Mary and I were preparing to leave together to visit dumpsters. Among scores of neighborhoods in America, there is a league of people, without benefit of a formal organization, who shop at the refuse bins. We glean wondrous items from its metal caverns and prefer to call it negative shopping, although my friends in another neighborhood refer to the place as 'The Store'. We remove things that others have thrown out and put them to good use.

Mary's doorbell rang and she went to answer it. She escorted a young man into the living room.

"Dee, this is Jane's son, my nephew, Jared. Jared, this is my good friend Dee," Mary said.

"Hello," I said, searching for something to say.

Jared wore a casual suit, no tie, and expensive looking walking shoes. His aftershave gave off a slight smell of wood.

"Should he be here, Mary?" I asked.

"It's okay, Dee. He's not staying in the area for long. He wanted to meet me in person," Mary said.

Jared didn't stay long. He was polite, handsome with light skin, blue eyes, and blond hair. He appeared similar in some ways to his mother. Mary answered his questions about her family and life and then he got up to leave.

"I must go, Aunt Mary. I appreciate your willingness to see me. We won't meet again, but I will keep you in my thoughts," he said.

"And I will you, Jared. Take care and live your life to the fullest. You deserve it," Mary said.

They hugged as Jared left. Mary closed the door looking thoughtful as she came back in the room.

"Nice young man, huh," Mary said. "I couldn't tell him."

"I know. He'll be okay. He's the one I saw at the grocery store that day, Mary. I'm sure of it," I said.

"I know. He told me about that. He was afraid he frightened you," she said.

"Well, duh. Oh well. That's water over the spillway, huh. He does seem nice, though," I said.

"Yes, he is, and is not a threat to anyone. Time to shop, I say. Let's get the heck out of here," Mary said.

Chapter Twenty-Eight

Our days returned to the usual and uneventful life after the encounters with Damon and his disreputable and dangerous cohorts.

Janet is in contact with me every week from Tucson and is dating a gentleman. Mary and I are discussing a bus trip to see her in the spring. Mary has found renewed vigor by walking and going to the pool often to exercise and has discussed her budget with me and without regret regarding its limits. She is seeing a man who is a person I regard as a good match for her.

Winter Gardens remains the same with the changes you'd expect. There are new people moving in every month and others who go to live elsewhere. Moving trucks pull in and out, the emergency vehicles arrive often carrying away the people I've learned to love, or those I've learned not to trust. If there are moving vans coming in, often there are furniture store delivery trucks on the premises the following week. Grocery store and bottled water deliveries are common, likewise the package delivery trucks. The resident's bus continues to take residents to doctor and hair appointments for those who no longer drive.

Coffee time revealed a few interesting tid-bits.

"Did you guys know that The Terminator left all her belongings when she left?" Gloria asked.

"No. How'd you find out?" said, John the resident's expert coffee maker.

"There was a van parked outside the building where she lived and I watched them loading up furniture. Clothes, too," she answered.

"Kinda shows to go ya what kind of person she was, huh?" John said.

"Can you imagine the kind of stuff the manager and owners have to put up with in this place? I mean, really. What a pain. They have to pay to get that stuff hauled away, I'm sure," I said.

"They gotta get it outa there so they can clean it up for the next renter," John said.

"Oh. And Myrtle Fry, the old gal in 509 tried to paint her wall in the living room by herself. Guess she was standing on a chair to reach up higher, she slipped, and her foot caught the paint bucket and spilled it all over herself, the wall, and one of her living room chairs," Gloria added.

"What a mess that must have been. I bet she'll have to pay to get it cleaned up," I said.

"And get this. The paint was deep purple," Gloria said.

"No. That is just too much," I said, barely able to keep from laughing out loud.

"Well, in retrospect, it is pretty funny," Gloria said.

It wasn't long before the both of us had a good laugh together. John is so serious. He didn't think it was funny.

Our maintenance staff of two continues to take care of our requests, replacing bulbs, dried up plastic vertical blinds, furnace filters, and fixing jammed disposal units. They are courteous and most often cheerful. We have learned that if they come together, it is because they don't know you well. It can also mean they are protecting themselves from the women who proposition any man who crosses their threshold. If one of them shows up, then you have earned their trust. I am not aware of what the unwritten rules are for male residents who generate work orders.

Martha and Barney moved this past week. She rang my doorbell one day and greeted me with her usual acerbic banter.

"Did you see the garbage in the elevator? Some stupid person spilled blueberries and didn't pick them up.

It's a mess. See this squished junk all over the bottom of my shoes? I won't come in your place. I don't want to get it on your carpet," she said.

"Martha. Take off your shoes and hand them over. I bet I can rinse them off in the sink,"

"Well, all right," she said, bending over to remove them, passing gas as she did so.

"Nobody ever tells ya you can't control those damn noises when you get old, do they," she said.

I don't think she was embarrassed, but she wanted to acknowledge that she'd made the noise. She handed me her shoes and I rinsed them and took a paper towel to pick off the pieces of berry that remained stubborn to get rid of. I wiped them dry and handed them back to her.

"I came to say goodbye, Dee," she said, as she put her shoes back on, once, again releasing a toot.

"Sorry, sorry," she said. This time I think she was self-conscious.

"Why are you and Barney leaving?" I asked.

"You know, maybe you don't know, Barney's been acting strange. Can't tell you how often I've found him wandering in the halls in his underwear and he can't tell me where he thinks he's going. Poor old man. It's time for us to live somewhere he'll be safe. We've been together a mighty long time and I don't want to take a chance he'll go out in the night and get himself killed," she explained.

"Besides the hall wandering, he has other problems. His doctor told us they can't do anything more for him. His heart, you know. Now doesn't that beat all hell? How many 80 year olds here have heard the same damned thing? They don't want to spend time or money on the oldies that they figure have one foot in the grave," Martha lamented. "What, you turn 80 and it's toodleloo, nice to see you, wouldn't want to be you?" she added.

"I've heard that from others too, Martha. Pretty sad. Keep asserting yourself. Guess I don't have to tell you that, huh?" I remarked.

"Well, it's been nice knowing you. You were always polite to me,"

"You'll be missed Martha. You've always given everyone a lot to think about," I said.

"Yes, well, do you want to know where we're going?" she asked with the accusing tone to which I'd grown accustomed.

"Of course. Let me get my address book," I answered.

Martha gave me the complete information regarding the facility where they were going. Three meals a day in the dining room, a movie theater, activities galore, bedding changes, and housekeeping services once a week.

"This sounds like the best place for both of you. Complete with a movie theater. How nice," I said.

"The movie theater has cushy lounge seats, too," she exclaimed.

"Perfect. Thanks for the address. I will visit."

"Call first," she ordered.

"Of course. Happy days, Martha," I said as she exited.

***

Mary and I traveled to Tucson and Janet and her new man friend treated us like royalty. The bus trip was easy and I loved seeing the scenery on the way. We spent long hours in the pool catching up on each of our activities.

"Tell me about this man friend of yours, Mary?" Janet asked.

"I met him at the cafeteria in the building where I go to my support group. He's a retired engineer, a widower, and lives in the west valley," Mary answered.

"I don't see much of Mary anymore, because of him. It's all good, though. Look how happy she is," I added.

"I noticed a glow about you the minute you came to my door. Any permanent plans with him, or what do you see for the future?" Janet asked.

"We're friends. Neither of us wants marriage," Mary answered.

"Friends with benefits, I hope," Janet said.

"Yes. Benefits. Funny way of putting it. I will tell you we enjoy each other tremendously," Mary said.

"Wow. That is terrific. I am happy for you. You have been through a great deal and you came out on the positive end. Tell me. Did either of you find out any more about Jane?" Janet asked.

Mary and I exchanged a quick glance.

"It remains a mystery," Mary answered.

Janet seemed satisfied with her answer. We continued to splash around in her pool, teasing and poking fun at each other and putting our relationships back in order.

The bus trip back to Daystar was uneventful. We were both sleepy because of the long days and evenings spent reminiscing and polishing off a few bottles of excellent Italian wines.

***

Tilly has been calling me often. Even though she's several years my senior, we find interesting topics to discuss. I am a regular on her patio in the evenings, sharing a glass of iced tea. She often brings up the story of the palm tree man, giggling about it. Then it turns into a somber reflection as she realizes again and again the reasons he chose that spot as a bed.

"Terrible, what some humans endure in their lifetime. I hope he received help that included good meals and a comfortable bed. My, my, how thin he was. A shame," she lamented.

"Tilly, you've been sending money to the shelter where they took him. I'm sure that changed his life," I said.

"I hope so. Now, my dear, you must make plans to come to dinner with me and my son next month. He's coming for a visit and I'm sure you two would get along," Tilly said.

"That's very nice of you Tilly, but I'm not an interesting conversationalist with younger folks," I said.

"He's not so young, dearie, pretty close to your age, I suspect."

"I would like to meet him. Good heavens. How old were you when you had him?"

"I was just eighteen. I was pregnant with him when John, my husband, was killed on his motorcycle."

"Oh. I'm sorry, Tilly. So, you raised him by yourself."

"Yes. He turned out rather well. He graduated college and went into private business."

"Guess it won't kill me to make conversation, then."

"No it wouldn't. Now you scoot home. I'm getting mighty sleepy. It is way past my bedtime," Tilly said.

It was eight o'clock. If you get up at five in the morning you'd want to be asleep by nine. Makes sense.

***

I met Tilly's son, Stephen, the following month. We went to a restaurant in northern Daystar known for its excellent Mexican food. The menu offered unfamiliar dishes and I'd not heard of several of them. I decided on something familiar; Chiles Relleno.

281

Stephen seemed like a nice enough person. He and his mother, Tilly, chatted among themselves, but also included me in their conversations. He indulged his mother with her endless stories of his youth, and didn't seem embarrassed by them. Our dinner hour filled up with good food and laughter.

The ride back to Winter Gardens remained quiet. I suspected Tilly had reached the end of her energy. Stephen asked if he could walk me back to my apartment after Tilly excused herself to retire for the evening. We walked and talked. I kept looking over at him. A handsome man and for some reason, familiar.

"Your mother mentioned you wanted to meet me. I assume because she and I have struck up a friendship," I said.

"More than that, Delores."

"Call me Dee, please."

"I wanted to meet you because I came across your name while I was on an assignment, and I realized you lived in the same complex as my mother."

"Oh. What kind of assignment?"

"Can I wait and explain it to you in private? It's a sensitive matter," he explained.

"Of course. You're welcome to come in, and we can talk there," I suggested.

"This is my first night here, Dee. I think I should get back to my mother's and make sure she's tucked in okay. She'll worry if I don't come back right away."

"I understand. She's a great gal, Stephen. I enjoy her spunk and admire her energy."

We stood on the sidewalk leading to the elevator. "I'll get your phone number from my mother and we'll arrange a place to meet, if you agree, and it's Steve," he said.

"Yes, I agree. I look forward to hearing from you, Steve," I said as he left.

As I lay in bed I realized I'd felt something I thought was dead long ago. When Tilly introduced her son and he greeted me with a voice, soft as velvet, yet assertive, I felt a twinge just below my breastbone. Dang. I'm interested in this man. He's pleasant looking, I'd say 5' 10" in height, has hair, at my age even knowing a nice man with hair is unusual, nice gray hair and he has good manners. Kind eyes. Likes his mother. Looks healthy, too.

He mentioned a sensitive matter. What would that be? I pay my taxes, don't have any debts that I'm aware of, and my children are fine. It better not be, Damon related.

***

My phone rang the next morning and it was Steve.

"I'm taking my mother to her doctor's appointment this morning. I should return by noon. I hoped you would let me take you to lunch," he said.

"That would be nice. I'll wait for your call," I answered.

"Tilly's test results are ready for her, and I want to be with her."

"I hope there's nothing serious going on," I said.

"We won't know until we see the results, but it is likely there is something," Steve said.

"I hope all goes well. I'll see you later," I said.

I sprang into action, going through my closet to see what I could wear that would be appropriate. Or look good. I haven't gone to lunch with a man for so long, I don't have any idea what to select.

I found one light-weight long skirt hanging in the back and I found a pretty blouse that looked as if it would go with it. However, in a darkened room with little lighting, the colors could change dramatically in the sunlight. I grabbed both pieces and walked out to my patio, looking to see if I had a match. Oh, yes. In the daylight it looked even better. Light blue floral on the top, plain blue skirt for the bottom. My sandals would do for footwear.

At twelve-thirty, Steve called and five minutes later he rang my doorbell.

"You look wonderful," he exclaimed.

"Thank you very much," I replied. "How did things go this morning?" I asked as we walked to the elevator.

"I'll explain in the car, Dee. I know there are ears listening. Mom told me how stories get out of proportion."

"So true."

"Which way to the Grecian Fountain restaurant?" Steve asked.

"Turn left here, go four blocks and turn right. Very good choice. They serve fresh, wonderful salads, if that's what you like."

"Nice and close and great salads. That's what Mom said."

We entered the overly cooled restaurant and the server directed us to a booth. I was happy I grabbed my lightweight sweater before we left.

My opinion on air-cooled restaurants is that manager's hope the clientele will eat and leave in the shortest time possible so the table can be turned for the next paying customer.

Steve opened the conversation as soon as the server brought our tea. "Mom is going to have a bit of a rough patch for a while. The biopsy on her lung showed some nodules and her doctor explained she has a type of pneumonia that needs treatment."

"That explains the coughing I've noticed lately. And I've noticed she tires faster than in previous months. Will she need to be hospitalized?"

"Not unless her condition doesn't improve with the medicines she prescribed. She is going to be 91, you know. I think that entitles her to be a little tired."

"You are right. I can check on her, if you like. To make sure she takes the medications on time and in the correct amounts. She's talked to me before about how much she hates even taking an aspirin."

"I'm glad you offered. That is my concern also. Thank you. I can't stay too much longer to see to it myself, unless I can lease a place for a few months."

"Your job doesn't require you to return soon?" I asked.

"I'm self-employed. I'm a private detective," he stated.

"Your story begins now, I think," I said smiling, although I felt reluctant to hear what would come next.

"I wanted to meet you, because I was hired by Jane McCarthy's son Jared to find his mother. I came across your name when I began investigating the motives of the group Damon Hereford belonged to."

"My name, why would my name come up? I have no German heritage," I said.

"No, but you are a close friend of Mary, and Mary is connected to Jane."

"Oh. I see, I guess. Funny, I never knew Damon's last name."

"You weren't close to him, so that follows. Anyway, Dee, the more I learned about you, and how you and your friends were doing your best to find Mary when she disappeared, the more I wanted to meet you. The Sheriff's department indicated all of you were instrumental in leading them to Mary's whereabouts, and consequently, squashing the efforts of that hare-brained fringe group. In addition, my mother thinks you are a great person. She goes on about how you put out that palm tree fire."

"I didn't completely extinguish it, you know."

"Enough so that nothing worse came of it."

"So, in all your investigating, did you find out what happened to Jane?" I asked.

"I was not privy to that. I believe you know why."

"I may have a pretty good idea about that." I smiled at Steve, and he looked at me as if he knew very well what I knew. And I thought I knew what he knew.

Chapter Twenty-Nine

At the end of May, I began to make plans to visit my children. I made my plane reservations and flew to northern climes when the summer heat began to stalk the desert and monsoon storms in the early evening hours dumped heavy rains into the vast dehydrated sands to the east of Daystar City.

Steve made plans to join me at my daughter's later in the month. We are seeing each other often and are under the scrutiny of busy eyes and the subject of conversation by motor mouths at Winter Gardens.

Once I arrived, the increase in humidity and the lower temps made outdoor excursions pleasurable. My daughter and son-in-law both work and I was on my own to entertain myself during the daytime hours.

Their home is large with two wings. On one side are two bedrooms, one of which is the master, and a large den with computers and printers located in-between. The other wing has two more bedrooms for guests. Their two older children occupied those rooms when they were youngsters, but they are now in college and living on their own in another state.

There is an air of freshness in the home supplied by an extraordinary heating and cooling system. These days have been cool and the outside air has provided the pleasant air.

On several occasions, I walked to town and enjoyed the quaint stores and art gallery displays. Some of the old buildings retain their original architecture and add to the feeling of treading where settlers first put down their roots. The library is close enough for me to use, and the outdoor cafes beckoned me with their colorful displays of food offerings.

The summer breezes and increased humidity give off grass-like odors unlike the ocean smells the wet desert produces. I enjoy the differences.

I went to the cafe on the corner of Vine and Prosperity and sat at a table under an umbrella. The server who came to my table took my order for a glass of iced tea with lemon.

"Do you want to order lunch, or is it just iced tea today?" she asked.

"I would like a menu, thanks," I answered.

She brought the tea with the menu. "Do you have any favorites?" I asked, referring to the short list of offerings.

"The chicken salad is good. Better than any other places that serve it," she replied. Her tone was cold and unfeeling.

"Let me take a minute to decide," I said, unable to put my finger on what was niggling at the back of my mind. I watched her move away from the table. She walked with a hint of defiance. I figured she didn't like her job and was waiting for something better to do. Not sure what that would be in this small town. I read and reread the menu, deciding on the chicken salad.

Ten minutes passed. My iced tea glass was three quarters empty. I looked around for the person who took my tea order. Another server approached my table.

"I'm sorry," she began. "The waitress became ill and had to go home. Are you ready to order?" she asked.

"Yes. I'll have the chicken salad sandwich please, on pumpernickel rye,"

"Chips or fries?"

"Neither. I'd like fruit if you have it?" I asked.

"No problem. It will be a few minutes," she said as she took the menu I handed her.

It wasn't long until she delivered my order. The sandwich was delicious and the fruit juicy and fresh.

I left the small establishment satisfied and sleepy. I headed toward my daughter's home.

***

Life in a small town, and living in a residence as opposed to an apartment complex has extreme differences. My daughter's home is located on a spacious lot surrounded by trees that block the view of neighbor's homes. It is quiet, peaceful, and seldom if ever, interrupted by sirens that signal impending problems. The town offers gathering places in the form of bars, restaurants, microbreweries, and theater, to meet and exchange gossip and information. I am excited to bring Steve to the venues offering various kinds of entertainment.

Steve called after I rested to let me know he was on his way from the airport in a van that would deposit him at the front door.

He arrived safely and brought his bag to the guest room where I was staying.

"Flight good?" I asked.

"Yes, it was. There was an interesting group of passengers on my flight," he answered.

"What made them interesting?"

"There were different cultures and skin colors represented. And two old men who conversed in Italian non-stop."

"Could you understand what they were saying?"

"Only a little. Wasn't anything I needed to know," he answered.

"Let's get you settled," I offered.

I hung his shirts and he put his other things in the drawer I'd left empty.

"Would you like some iced water? We can relax out on the patio, if you like," I suggested.

"Perfect."

The view of the 100's of pines and the soft music they produce with the wind rustling their needles is enough to relax the most hyperactive person. Occasional boulders interrupt the grand expanse of the lawn and at the yard's border is a salt lick to encourage deer to wander in and stay a while.

"My daughter and her husband will be home around 5:00 after work. I've put some chicken in a marinade in the frig so it can be put on the barbeque."

"Sounds wonderful. So, how are you doing with all this space to relax in?" Steve asked.

"I'm loving the change. I do miss the swimming pool, though," I answered. "More importantly, how are you doing now that Tilly is gone?"

"I miss her, of course. But the pneumonia came on so quickly and she was miserable. It is a relief to know she's no longer suffering. She lived a long and terrific life. I'm sure you felt the same way when your Mom died," Steve answered.

"Still miss her though. Did you manage to get everything out of her place?"

"Yes. The consignment store took most of the furniture. She had some really nice pieces. The rest I packed up and donated."

"Oh, I hear a car door close. Come on, and I'll introduce you," I said as I heard the front door open.

My daughter and son-in-law, Brenda and Bill are experienced hosts as they have gatherings in their home each month. They served cocktails and munchies to us on the patio and we talked and waited for the grill to heat.

Supper turned out well and both my daughter and her husband engaged in lively conversation with Stephen, so I knew they liked him right away.

Steve and I spent the week going to the small shops and galleries in town. One night we went to a movie, on another, we went to a production written by a local playwright.

When we stopped at the cafe for lunch, the server, who went missing the first time I was there, waited on us. We placed our order and sipped on our beverages.

"Did you notice the two men at the back table? Those are the same two that were on my flight," Steve said.

"Oh. No, I didn't notice."

Our food came and we ate in silence as we reveled in the beauty of the surrounding mountains.

When the waitress came to give Steve the bill, she flicked her blond hair several times. A nervous tick? Not sure why, but I looked down at her feet. She looked as if she was poised to walk toward the door. Not only that, she touched her nose every time she spoke. I had a funny feeling in my stomach.

Steve paid the bill and seemed to be in a hurry. He took my arm and hustled me out the cafe's door. He kind of pushed me into walking quickly and when we reached the corner, he turned to face me.

"Something is off. Did you feel it?"

"Yes I did. The waitress. I think it's Jane," I said.

"I believe the two Italian men are mob. I didn't get a good look at them on the plane, but at the restaurant, one of them took off his dark glasses. He is one of the men I was tailing in Phoenix. I'm sure. We need to warn her," he said.

"I agree. How are we going to do it?"

Steve had never acknowledged to me that he knew of Jane's circumstances, and I never told him what Mary said to me in confidence. We had an unspoken understanding of it.

"Here's how." Steve related his plan to me. "We must hurry."

We got back to the house and fast, without breaking any speed limits, to make arrangements. We took a cab to the rental agency, picked up the car, and drove toward the cafe. Steve let me off so I could walk in by myself.

The place was full of afternoon shoppers. The smell of grilled hamburgers and fries filled the air. I was relieved when the object of our plans waited on me once again.

"I'd like iced tea again," I said. I slipped a note inside the menu, handed it to her and smiled. "Please don't panic. I want you to read my note inside the menu as soon as you go back to the kitchen. Then go to the back door where the man I was with earlier will be there to take you to safety. I know who you are and you will be okay, I promise," I said. I used the clenched teeth method I'd done for so long with my broken jaw, in an attempt to be sure no one could read my lips. Hopefully, this time, she realized who I am.

The woman's eyes widened, there was a hint of recognition, and she pulled in a deep breath and relaxed again. She left my table and went into the kitchen.

I waited for fifteen minutes, nervous as all hell. Steve was at the rear entrance of the cafe waiting for Jane to come out the door. I had no way of knowing if she heeded my instructions. I noticed the two men were still at the table toward the back of the room. I did my best to seem relaxed and unhurried. How long had they been there? Most people don't stay that long. Maybe they're waiting for her to complete her shift. Not good.

I got up and went to the counter and asked the yawning clerk if I could have a glass of iced tea. "I think my waitress forgot I am here," I explained.

"Oh, ya. Sure. Be right with you," he replied.

I drank and sipped for a long while. I assumed everything had gone as planned because Steve had not returned to the cafe for me. After twenty minutes, I figured it was okay to leave the place.

I walked along the main street and went inside each of the stores checking my cellphone often to see if there were any messages. I was getting exhausted, walking, wondering, and traipsing in and out of each and every store. I did my best to look at things, fingering fabrics, picking up jars of this and that, trying to look as if I was deciding what to buy. I did see some lovely peach colored candles shaped like twisted bark. They would go well with the decor in my daughter's bedroom, so I bought a pair. Ye gads. They weren't cheap, but the price and the time it took to find them ticked off important minutes.

I decided to turn up one of the side streets and walk to the small square with park benches. I sat for some time with my eyes closed, happy there was a cool breeze to keep me comfortable. There were two other benches occupied. A couple with two small children who skipped around to the delight of their parents, and one old man with a cane who looked as if he was snoozing.

A food truck came driving up and parked nearby. The aroma of Mexican spices swirled about. Had I eaten lunch? My stomach growled. Oh yes, I had. I just didn't remember it because we ate so fast and we were both preoccupied.

The couple with their children in tow walked up to the window of the food truck and made a purchase. The kids jumped up and down while they waited for their tacos.

It had been two and a half hours since Steve dropped me off. Finally, my phone indicated a text message.

"Everything went as planned. Where are you?" he texted.

"At Farmer's Park on 2nd street, on a bench," I answered back.

"I'll be there shortly," he told me.

I breathed a sigh of relief. When he pulled up in the rental car, I couldn't have been happier if I'd been informed I'd won the Publisher's Clearing House Sweepstakes. I got into the car and turned to face Steve, who wore the same kind of grin I did.

"You did it. You got her to safety."

"Yup. Sheriff's Department was lucky to find a place for her on such short notice," he answered.

"Did she speak to you?"

"She seemed on edge. Can't blame her there. But, after speaking with a deputy, she thanked me for getting her away from what could have been a bad situation. She's wasn't very talkative."

"Now what?"

"We'll have to wait for her new identity to come through. I volunteered to take her to the airport once she has it. The rented car will work for that too," Steve said.

"Okay. We'll wait. In the meantime, we'll have some explaining to do to my daughter," I said.

"Why don't you let me handle it. I can hide a lot of the pertinent facts and your knowledge of them behind my private investigator status."

"Oh. Good idea. I like that."

***

"My black wig?" Brenda asked. "Whatever for?"

"I can replace your sunglasses, but I don't know about the wig," I said.

"Don't give it a thought. Someone gave it to me, so it is not a big loss," she said.

I let Steve explain the situation. "So you see, we had to get her out of there."

"Wow. That's some story. No wonder you both look wide-eyed and exhausted," she said. "Bill should be home shortly. Why don't you two go out on the patio and relax, and I'll mix up the cocktails."

Brenda returned with a tray filled with snacks and iced gin and tonic drinks, her husband, Bill joining her.

"I hear you two have had quite a day. So, you're a private detective. Guess you never know what kind of people or circumstances you are going to run into," Bill said.

"You are so right. At least today, I could get someone out of harm's way," Steve said.

"A toast to you, then," Bill said as he raised his glass.

I smiled and appreciated the deft way this lovely man told the story without getting my name involved except as an accessory after the fact.

"What will happen now? Will she be able to get out of the state, or what?" Brenda asked.

"Yes, the authorities will see to that," Steve said.

"Well, all's well that ends well," Bill said.

Chapter Thirty

A week passed and we hadn't received a word about Jane's documents. On the eighth day, the phone rang at my daughter's residence. It was Saturday and both she and her husband Bill were at home.

"It's for Steve, Mom," she called out.

Steve answered it and came into the dining room where we were finishing our breakfast.

"I have to go and tend to some business. I'd like you to go with me, Dee, if that is okay?" Steve asked.

"Sure. Give me a minute to find my lipstick and purse and I'll be with you," I answered.

"What's up," I asked Steve when we pulled out of the driveway in Brenda's car.

"Gotta go rent a car again. All the documents have been delivered and it's time for me to take her to the airport," Steve reported. "I'm to meet the Sheriff at the abandoned airstrip. Do you know where that is?"

"Uh, not exactly. Let me see if I can find it on one of the maps on my phone. Hang on." I searched and there it was. "Okay. You need to take Central out 5 miles north, hang a left on airport lane and that should get you there."

"Got it. You take Brenda's car and go to back to their house after you drop me off. I'll text you when my mission is complete."

"I can't come with?"

"Sheriff's says, no. Sorry. Could be risky."

"Why?"

"We don't know whether those men have information about where she is, or not," Steve explained.

"I see. Well, tell her I wish her the best."

"Will do."

We arrived at the car rental place and Steve went inside the small building. The attendant drove a large sedan and parked it next to my daughter's car.

I waited in the car while Steve went inside to pick up the keys. When he reappeared, I got out and walked over to give him a hug. I saw movement from the side of the building on the outside.

"Oh crap." I said.

Steve grabbed my hand and we hauled our butts toward the rental car. I got in the driver's seat and Steve told me to "get in and keep your head down."

"I think you're the one who should crouch down," I said as I pressed my foot hard on the gas pedal spitting up gravel behind.

I drove out of the lot and onto the side street.

"Now what?" I asked.

"Hang on Dee. Just keep driving. I'm calling 911."

"What's going on?"

"Two men came out from the side of that building. Looked a lot like those two Italians to me," he answered.

"Oh, no. What are we gonna do?"

"Sit tight, sweetie. I'll get instructions from the Sheriff. We've got enough of a head start. I don't see them behind us yet."

"Your Mom used to call me sweetie."

"Ya."

I could hear him giving his location to the operator.

"They're catching up," I heard him say.

Then the motor roared as I sped through the town's side streets.

"Glad you got a big car with a big engine," I said.

"Hmm." Then he said, "How far till I'm there?" then a pause. "Okay, we turn where? Got it."

I figured he was still talking to the 911 operator.

"You're going to have to make some evasive maneuvers. They're getting closer."

That's when I heard shots ring out. Sounded like they zinged past my ear, that's how close.

"They're shooting at us, for God's sake," I hollered.

"The car swayed side to side as I turned the steering wheel back and forth. Steve and I were being jerked this way and that and I got knocked in the ribs by the door opener. I did my best not to groan. I knew Steve had enough to pay attention to and I didn't need to add any drama.

The tires screeched as I turned one way and then another in quick succession. Then I was tossed up a few inches in the air as the car hit a large bump in the road. I landed hard and I gave out a grunt. There were a lot of large holes and bumps in the road and I gave out several more grunts.

"You okay?" Steve asked.

"Yes. You do what you do, never mind about me." Never mind that I think I'm going to end up in a bunch of messy pieces that even a puzzle expert couldn't put back together.

"We don't have much more time to get there, Dee. You've got to go faster. Sheriff'll take her back to the safe house if we don't get there on time," Steve said.

"Okay," I said as I pushed harder on the gas pedal. I scared myself with the added speed.

Steve told me to make a hard left and we continued on a gravel road, the tires growling as we sped past farms and groves of trees. I figured I could spit up plenty of rocks and dust to blur the vision of our pursuers.

Bumps and holes continued to come up and went on for several minutes when all of a sudden I saw Sheriff cars directly in front of us. I hit the brakes, tossing us both forward.

Steve got out of the car shouting instructions for me to stay where I was. I heard him run.

Oh gad. I'm by myself in here. I decided this was the time for me to crouch down. The urge to sit up and look was overwhelming. However, any movement produced painful twinges I didn't wish to keep doing to myself.

Right then, another car drove up and came to a quick stop. The engine was still going and I heard a car door open. It must be located a few yards ahead. Then there was a lot of yelling. 'Come out of there with your hands up, and all the familiar phrases you hear on the TV cop shows.

Those som'bitches that chased us are parked near me. What if they get out with their guns and fire into the seat where I am?

A whole bunch of gunfire ensued. Dah, dat, dat, dat, dat, dat. Then, dead quiet. I listened hard and I heard feet scuffling across the gravel. I dared to bring my head up far enough to look out the window. A uniformed man was standing with his back toward my windshield. He had a gun in his hand, pointed toward the ground. I am open mouthed, wide eyed, and highly agitated. This is not a TV cop show. This is for real.

Steve pulled open the car door and told me I could get out. It took some time to unsquish my cramped legs and slide out. I fell into his waiting arms.

"They're both dead, right?" I asked.

"Yes, and all the good guys are safe," Steve answered, patting my back with a soothing gesture. I needed about another good half hour of those soothing gestures.

A few minutes went by and Steve and I got back into the car. This time, I was in the passenger seat. He maneuvered the car around the Sheriff's vehicle and parked under a shade tree, facing out.

"You okay? You look kind of pale?" he asked.

"Just your normal human being reaction to nearby gun fire and dead persons. I'll calm down, in a little while," I answered.

"Okay. I'll be back in a minute. Nothing more is going to happen, I assure you," he said as he exited our rental vehicle.

Good. I needed a minute alone to breathe deeply and reassess my feelings. I never in my life have had an experience like this. I've dealt with emergency situations but not a life and death chase. And real people with real flesh and blood being shot to death in such close proximity. Ugh.

When he returned, he had Jane by his side. She was carrying the luggage with clothing inside that we'd provided.

Steve put her luggage in the trunk and stayed at the side of the car while she got in the back seat.

"I'm cleared to leave and get this woman to where she belongs," Steve said to me. "You look as if you are okay now. And you, dear lady, did a great job driving this behemoth of a car without any hesitation. I think you have no fear," he commented.

I knew from experience that fear comes to me after a bad situation, not during, when I mull over the possibilities of what could have happened. So far, I hadn't begun to shake or tremble inside.

I turned toward Jane and said, "Hello, again. I think your worries are, how can I put this, out of the picture for good."

Jane nodded without a verbal response.

All of us buckled our seatbelts and Steve began to drive away from the deadly scene.

"Where was she when all this went down?" I asked.

"A second patrol car was back quite a ways and out of site with Jane inside," Steve answered.

"Guess they were prepared for anything that might happen. Were those the same men you spotted in the cafe?" I asked.

"Yes. They won't be bothering anyone ever again," Steve answered.

"Are you taking me back to the rental place?" I asked.

"Nope. You're okay to go with me," he said grinning like a kid riding a new bike.

We drove in silence for several miles. Then I turned toward the back seat.

"Jane, I want you to know that I met your son at Mary's not too long ago. He seems like a fine young man. You can be very proud," I said.

Jane pushed her lower lip hard against her lower teeth. It seemed she was acknowledging the truth of my statement.

"I'm sorry you have to keep relocating. It must be a difficult trying to get reestablished in a new community," I said.

"I do all right for myself," Jane said.

"Is there anything you want me to tell Mary?" I asked.

She was quiet for several seconds. I noticed a tear sliding down her cheek.

"No, nothing. Well, yes there is. She was the only person in that lousy complex that would give me the time of day. Turns out, we're related. Ain't that the weirdest thing you ever heard? And she's nice. Unique. Not like the others. Not that you're like them. I don't know you. Tell her, oh, I don't know. Tell her I'll be fine and I'll always think kindly of her," Jane answered.

"I can do that," I said.

"Did Mary tell my son, well, what's up with me?" Jane asked.

"No, she didn't," I answered.

There was no further conversation after that until we dropped her off at the curb by the airport.

"Thank you both for all you done. I'm so grateful, believe me," she said as she turned away and walked to the outdoor check-in kiosk.

Steve and I waited until she disappeared behind the glass doors to the terminal before we left the area. She did not turn around to see if we were still there.

Neither of us spoke all the way back to the car rental office, which was an hour's drive. I closed my eyes and begged for relief from the ache in my side.

When we returned to my daughter's car, Steve took my hand and drew me close. "Do you want to go over to that park and talk about all this?" he asked.

"Good idea. But, stop at the drugstore. I need some pain pills. Those humps in the road did a number on my body," I said.

"Oh. I'm so sorry. Couldn't be helped. Damn those lowlifes. They sure messed up our plans," Steve lamented.

We settled on one of the park's benches under the shade of a grand old maple tree, leafed out in glorious fashion with numerous branches hovering above us. I swallowed a couple of aspirin with a swig from the water bottle we purchased.

"I guess we could both fill in the other about what we know. I'll start," I said to Steve. "Mary and I went into Jane's apartment the day after she was taken by ambulance to a location unknown to us. We were looking for something Jane asked Mary to get if anything ever happened to her. Two men came in while we were there. We hid in the storage room off the patio. Have no idea who they were."

"FBI," Steve said.

"Scared the beegeebers out of us. Mary found a notebook Jane kept. Looking through it later, we found information about her family and the death of her husband. Oh no. She didn't marry him. He was mob. Jared was their son. She was supposed to testify in court because she witnessed her, uh, significant other's murder, but she was threatened numerous times by the mob. She must have testified though. Did she?"

"Yes. Afterward she was given a new identity, and a few minor plastic surgeries. She gave up her son for adoption. She told the authorities she couldn't handle hiding even with her new identity and wondering if they would ever be safe, and she thought going it alone would be easier," Steve said.

"So, how did you come in to all of this?" I asked.

"This last year, someone came to me asking for help to find the whereabouts of his mother. It was Jared. He gave me a rather sketchy account of his early childhood with her and I realized what must have happened. The FBI filled me in on the rest."

"So you watched and learned stuff?"

"Sorta like that. The FBI notified the local Sheriff's Department about Jane's so called abduction. She was rescued, you know, so they could relocate her. Then Mary was taken after Kathleen's family reported Kathleen missing. Those two being from the same complex and since my Mother lived there, I couldn't help but be interested. I got up to date on all of that, and that's how I became familiar with your name. My Mom filled me in on what kind of a person you were."

"All of that was complicated, huh. Only one more thing. Did you know what Jane was referring to when she asked if Mary told Jane's son 'what's up with me'?" I asked.

"No."

"She's very ill. Has maybe six months to live," I said. "Mary didn't see the value in telling Jared," I explained.

"There are excellent medical facilities where she's headed. I bet her handlers are seeing to her care," Steve said.

"Can you tell me where that is?"

"Nope."

"I can understand that. Hey. I just remembered something I forgot to tell you. This is funny. About six different people confessed to us they were responsible for Jane's death."

"No kidding. That is bizarre."

"Kept us entertained. Janet kept saying 'no body, no crime,' but people owned up to bumping her off anyway. I must say, Jane looks pretty good considering her health condition. She looks better as a blonde than the red head she was at Winter Gardens," I said. "Well, she must have had a little more plastic surgery, too. I didn't recognize her until I remembered how she sort of posed while she talked, and how she flipped her hair."

"I just thought of something else. Boy. A light just dinged in my head. Steve Bauer, son of Tilly Bauer. Your mother was one of the TCOA targets. That's how you got involved."

Steve smiled. "How'd you figure that out?"

"Two things. I took a note off the table in that house I climbed in. I didn't look at it right away, but now I remember what it said. It was a list. Last item on it said, 'one more to get - 'Bau' the last letters were smudged. I didn't put it together until now. The other thing; it was you with Jane the last night she was seen. I saw it on the digital record from the surveillance camera. The pictures were grainy and it was hard to look at, but I memorized the face of the man she was with that last night. Were you taking her out to give her a strategy for her faked death?"

"You could say that," he said, now smiling broadly.

"There's something else we gals couldn't figure out. How did those men get Jane's belongings out of there without anyone hearing or seeing anything?"

"It was easy, actually, Dee. They had a passkey to a storage room located on the same floor. She didn't have much in there in the way of furniture. They were there in the darkest hours of the night when they knew most residents would be asleep. They took her clothing and personal items with them and left."

"I didn't know there was a storage room up there. No wonder nobody saw or heard anything. Mary told me she had one of those fancy guest beds, a blow up one, but it has a fold up frame. I guess that would be easy enough to haul out of there. I bet they exited through the stairs instead of using the elevator too," I said.

"Don't know, but that sounds reasonable. Less chance of running in to anyone," Steve said.

I stood up from the bench and stretched. "Wow. All of this is between you and me. I can't tell my family any of it. This has been a day to remember. We'd better get back to my daughter's. We only have a couple more days to be here," I said.

CHAPTER THIRTY-ONE

Brenda and Bill greeted us on the patio with looks of anticipation and a large pitcher of iced tea. We filled our glasses and sat on the expensive well-padded chairs.

"You both look tired. Did everything go well?" Bill asked.

"Yes. My job is complete and Dee helped a great deal."

"I did? I thought I was added complication," I remarked.

"Don't believe that for a second," Steve said.

"I suppose because of your line of work, you can't give us any details," Bill said.

"You're right." Steve paused and looked over at me.

"How much longer are you going to be doing this Steve? Any plans to retire?" I asked.

"Guess this is as good a time as ever to tell you. One of the reasons I came here was to tell you I am retiring. My last day was today." I am officially retired as of eight am tomorrow morning."

"Really? How's that?" I asked.

"I've sold my business, files and all, to a young man who is well qualified to take up where I left off," Steve said

My mouth was hanging open. I closed it and thought about what he'd just said.

"Terrific," the only remark that came to mind.

"Now you and I can go ahead with some of the ideas we've been discussing." Steve said, smiling.

"And that would be?" Brenda asked, eyebrows raised high.

"We're both planning on moving. Not sure exactly where, but there will be a change of scenery for sure," Steve answered.

"I had no idea it was going to be this soon, though," I added.

"I do hope you will keep us well informed," my daughter said. She had a small smile.

"Of course. You'll be the first to know. I have a lot of researching to do first." I said. "I'm not sure how another location will fit into my budget.

"I know how you love to look up everything on the computer. I'm sure your research will give you the information you want," Brenda said.

"Absolutely. My favorite thing to do." I finished my glass of tea and set it on the table. "I am in need of a nap,

I'm sure you understand. Don't let me sleep any longer than an hour, okay?" I asked.

"We'll be fine without you Dee. Steve and I are going to play a game of chess," Bill said.

***

The next two days passed by faster than I would have liked. Brenda and Bill took those days off work to spend time with us. They rented a pontoon and we went out on one of the nearby lakes. A beautiful, warm sunny day joined us and the views were spectacular. A few jet skis whizzed past us as well as water skiers. Bill maneuvered the boat to stay well out of their way. Steve and I were rested by this time and we both realized that my family had accepted Steve into their lives. The next day we hiked in the woods outside of the town where they resided. The trees were in full summer bloom and provided a canopy from the hot summer sun above us.

Steve and I left for the airport in a shuttle bus after saying long goodbye's to my daughter and her husband.

"By the time we get back to Daystar I should have confirmation that her handler took Jane to a clinic where she will get the medical attention she needs," Steve said.

"You can't tell me where she went, huh," I said.

"Nope. She'll be well taken care of. I am surprised they took a chance on a small town like this."

"Ya. And of all the places where she could have been, I came to visit here. And then you. What are the chances?" I said.

"It was her good fortune, for sure," Steve said.

"You sure do have the connections," I said. "Seemed like the Sheriff here had no problem handling your requests and backing you up when you needed it," I commented.

"It pays in my business to be honest and forthcoming with information whenever the authorities need it. They pay it back in spades, I can tell you," he answered.

***

Circumstances at Winter Gardens didn't change much in the time I was absent. Steve is staying at his Mother Tilly's place and I am remaining in my rental for the time being.

Mary and I had dinner together at my place and she filled me in on her activities.

"I'm still going to therapy, but now it seems I'm more help to others in the group than I ever imagined I'd be able to do," she told me.

"Now, why would you say that? You have always been the person of reason and full of helpful advice when people need it." I commented.

"Yes, but a lot has happened to me. I don't think I'm the same person," Mary said.

"Change is inevitable, Mary. Your change has been for the good. All of us hope positive changes will happen during our lives," I said.

"One good thing, the dreaded white van hasn't been here since you left."

"Great. No one died, so no need for the coroner."

"Nope."

"How are things going with your beau?" I asked.

"Really good, thanks. We see each other enough but not so much that we get tired of each other. It's hard to adjust to another person in your life after all those years alone," she said. "How about you?"

"Steve is great. He's renting his Mom's unit month to month until he decides what he wants to do next, and where," I said.

"You'll go where he goes, won't you?"

"I don't know. He hasn't mentioned anything about that," I answered.

"You'd be smart to hang to that one, Dee. He's a keeper,"

"Yes, I agree."

Coffee time still occurs around ten in the morning, the activities are ongoing without the benefit of a director, the pool is well attended especially on the mornings when there is a water aerobic exercise class, and birthdays are celebrated once a month with cake and ice cream.

Mary and I elected to go to coffee together today. Residents new to the complex filled up the chairs and the rest were those I'd known since I moved in.

'Where are you originally from?' 'how long have you been here?' 'do you play Hand & Foot?' 'is there Bingo here?' and 'how often do they raise the rent?' questions were tossed about the room like a ping pong ball bouncing off the table.

The conversations remained lively until one little dark-haired woman stood and began to speak. "My name is Gloria. I've been here for a month. My husband died a week ago," she pronounced.

Murmurs of condolences came from the new residents, and Gloria sat down again. Mary and I both know

323

she's been living here for over a year and her husband died shortly after she moved in. I'm sympathetic to her situation, but I can't help but think her bran muffin isn't done in the middle. Other than her memory shortages, she seems to do well.

Ron, the manager stepped out of his office and came over to the tables.

"How's everyone doing today?" he asked.

Positive answers filled the air.

"That's great. I have a nice surprise to tell you. The owners of this complex ordered a new bus and it will be delivered next month. We hired a full-time driver, who is well qualified, I might add, to be available for doctor appointments, grocery store runs and entertainment venues," he said.

A shout of joy went up in the room.

"There will be some new rules about using the bus. I will have copies available tomorrow and I want all of you to have them and read them. It is important that all of us follow the rules," Ron explained.

"What kind of rules?" someone asked.

"Well, here are a few. Riders must buckle up their seat belts before the bus leaves the complex, riders who have bathroom issues, need to use protection so that the bus seats remain clean and stain free for the next passenger, and here's one that you need to pay attention to. If you signed up to ride and don't show up and haven't informed us of your inability to be there, you will be fined $10.00 and it will show up on your next month's rent bill," Ron added.

"That seems reasonable to me," one resident commented.

"Who's got $10.00 to throw around?" another responded.

"How many rules are there?" someone asked.

"There are several. They are all meant to be followed so that the bus experience remains good for each and every resident," Ron answered.

"Who's the new driver?"

"You'll find out the first day the new bus is in service," Ron said.

Ron ended his announcement and came next to where I was seated. "Dee, we have been swamped with move-ins and move-outs. I wondered if you and Mary might be interested in extra earnings by helping us get some of the inventory cleaned?"

"Well, I guess I could consider that. Let Mary and I discuss it and I'll get back to you," I answered.

"Soon, please." Ron turned and went back to his office

"So, Dee, how come Steve is still in Tilly's place?" Darlene Madigan, the good-looking eighty year-old asks.

I barely had time to absorb Ron's question, much less pay full attention to what Dar asked.

"Umm, he's finishing up Tilly's estate things and deciding where he wants to live," I answered.

"Surely that would be with you?"

I blushed. "I don't know everything he thinks, Darlene Madigan," I answered.

Mary, Darlene and I continued to chat for a while. Before we left, I asked Mary what she thought about Ron's proposal.

"I'm sure I can handle that now, so long as it's not a whole bunch to clean. I could sure use the extra money," she answered.

"Okay then. I'll let him know," I said.

I was still tired from the last day's exercises in the pool. I over compensated for the time I was away and now I needed a rest.

Steve called later that afternoon and invited me out to dinner. It became what I'd call a supper; hamburgers and salad. We talked about how Tilly specified in her will that

Steve would inherit everything, money and all her possessions.

"How much of her things are you keeping?" I asked.

"Very little. She had some nice pieces of art and a couple of small sculptures I'm going to hang onto. I have the best of her furniture already. She gave it to me when she moved here," he answered.

"Mary and I are going to clean some of the rentals. Guess they have more than the usual number of folks moving in and out," I told him.

"Will you have time for me? I've been looking online at some other living situations. I think it would be fun to go look? Want to join me?" he asked.

"Sure. Always fun to see how the other half-lives. I'll make time," I answered.

CHAPTER THIRTY-TWO

Mary and I picked up the cleaning cart and vacuum from the management office and rolled it over to the ground floor apartment by the pool.

"Hey. This is Damon's old place," I remarked.

"Yep. Wonder if he left a mess?" Mary asked.

I unlocked the door and brought the cart in while Mary pushed the vacuum through the door. There was a light on and the vertical blinds closed, so I opened them.

"Well, not bad, just needs our TLC," I remarked.

"I'll start with the kitchen cupboards while you vacuum. Okay?" I asked.

I got up on the step stool and began washing the cabinets inside and out. About an hour later, Mary rushed into the kitchen. She looked perplexed and was shaking a bag in front of me.

"You're not going to believe this," she shouted.

"What?" I got down from the countertop.

"This. Look in here," she said, thrusting the paper bag at me.

I opened it and stared unbelieving at its contents. "What the hell? Where'd you find it? How much to you think is in here?" I asked.

"I was cleaning out the cabinet in the laundry area. One of the shelves was uneven and I tried to straighten it when I realized there was something under it causing it to tilt. I put everything I found in the bag here."

"We better check to see if there's any more," I said. We went to the cabinet and began removing each shelf.

"Ye gods. There's more. Let's go through the other shelves," I suggested.

By the time we finished collecting the money that was distributed throughout the apartment we were certain the total was in the thousands.

"Now what?" Mary asked.

"I'm taking this home and then I'll call Steve. He'll know what to do," I answered.

"Let's finish this up though. I want to get done and get the heck out of here," Mary said.

We worked for several more hours. The oven was as clean as a freshly bathed baby and we knew what we couldn't handle would be taken care of by the carpet cleaners and the painters.

We returned the cart and the vacuum cleaner to the storeroom and I went home with the bag of money.

I hit the cellphone pad with Steve's number. He didn't answer, so I left a voicemail for him to come over as soon as he could.

My recliner called out to me. I was exhausted. I turned on the TV and laid back. Minutes later, almost asleep, my ears caught the gist of a breaking news story.

"New developments in the story we brought you this month about the arrest of several members of a terroristic group known as TCOA. Another member has been identified as belonging to the group and is being sought for questioning. He is described as a 70-year-old male, 6 foot, graying short-cropped hair and noticeably discolored teeth. If you have any information as to the whereabouts of this individual, please contact the Central County Sheriff's department at–"

Ye gods. That sounds like Damon. I thought they arrested him. I am alarmed and wondering what to do. I tried Steve's phone once again, and still, no answer.

The footrest slammed hard back into the chair as I heaved myself out of it and went to my bedroom. I pulled out all my dirty laundry from the hamper, put the bag full of money into the bottom, and stuffed my clothes back into it on top of the money. I sort of felt like a burglar.

I paced back and forth in the living room hoping for a quick return call from Steve. Loud banging on my front door jarred me alert. I looked through the peephole and saw Damon standing there. How could this be?

I put the boot to keep out intruders under the doorknob. The bottle of pepper spray was in the letter holder at my front door. Then I called 911, put the phone down so I could grab the spray and yelled into the phone. "Help! I need help," I yelled my address, hoping the operator could hear me over the banging on my door. Knuckle banging was replaced by kicks to the door. The boot held.

Then a crack appeared in the molded plastic. It got larger as the kicks multiplied. Oh boy. I could see his whole body through the widened, gaping hole.

As soon as he broke through, I sprayed most of the pepper spray into his eyes and face. His entire body came through the door and I brought my knee up hard into his crotch. The somebitch fell on me, pushing all the oxygen out of my diaphragm in a whoosh.

There was a great deal of noise and commotion after that. I managed to get some air into my lungs but rolling his dead weight off me proved to be daunting. Someone in a uniform came to my rescue and I gasped as I felt the relief that came when his weight lifted off my tired old body.

Steve rushed to my side and helped me stand.

"I sure wish you'd been here after I first called you," I said fighting back tears.

"I was over in the East Valley. Never mind that. I called the Sheriff as soon as you called. I knew something was up by the sound of your voice. I didn't know about the person of interest they were looking for until I talked to them. Didn't take long to figure it out," Steve said.

"Figure what out?" I asked.

The Sheriff's deputies were working on Damon, waking him up, cuffing him and dragging him into the hallway.

"That, my dear, is Damon's brother. He's the one who attacked you, not Damon. A very bad individual. Wanted all over Arizona for armed robbery, he's a heavy drug user, and the enforcer for the TCOA. Also, he's the one who murdered Kathleen, according to the other members."

"They sure look alike. Except for the teeth. I took it for granted that it was Damon who attacked me."

I suddenly remembered the money.

"Wait! Get one of the deputies back in here," I requested.

I went to the bedroom, tossed out the dirty clothes, and retrieved the bag of money. "Here you go," I said to the deputy. "This is the money we found under shelves at Damon's," I explained.

"We were about to go there to look for it. Damon told us its location and said we should get it before his brother figured out where it was. It was stolen from convenience stores all over the state and was intended to be used to build up their organization. There's a reward for finding this individual and we will see to it that you get it," the deputy said.

"Huh. Such a deal." I'm 'way too exhausted to come up with something more grateful.

It seemed like hours passed before the hallway cleared, another door put on to replace the shattered hunk of molded plastic that proved to be no contest for a man of his determination and size.

Steve remained all the while and helped with the door's installation.

"Me, shower," I said, after everyone was gone.

"Staying."

"K."

"I Love you."

"Me too. Dinner?"

"Of course."

"Out?"

"Copy that."

The shower made me feel 100% better. I wrapped myself in a towel and exited the bathroom. I found Steve in my bedroom, in my bed, under the sheets. I thanked myself for changing them that morning.

"Oh boy," I said as I crawled in next to him. "Shower, you, and dinner. What more could a gal ask?"

The End

ABOUT THE AUTHOR

Lou Korus is retired and lives with her cat in Sun City, Arizona.

She is a former President of the Sandpoint Chapter of the Idaho Writers League, and a multiple award-winning author of short stories and poetry.

Lou has an extensive background in music and directed a women's choir for seventeen years.

Readers may access her website LouKorus.weebly.com or email her at: louidaho@hotmail.com

Other Books by Lou Korus

Death and Duplicity   ISBN: 978-0-9853906-2-4   2016

www.ingramcontent.com/pod-product-compliance
Lightning Source LLC
Chambersburg PA
CBHW060512180626
46817CB00002B/346